MW00466245

Katelyn Marie Peterson

2021, Amore Moon Publishing – TWB Press

For Justin Fritch, my rock.
Always and forever.

Cold Sweat

Edited by Terry Wright

Cover Art by Terry Wright

ISBN: 978-1-944045-96-8

Chapter 1

It was still dark outside when Isabel's nightmare startled her awake. Her hands were shaking, and she fought to catch her breath. The alarm clock read: *5:30 A.M.* She had no desire to go back to sleep. The nightmares had become more frequent and intense. Shuddering, she swung her legs off the bed, slipped into her purple slippers, and stagger-stepped into the kitchen of her cozy ranch home to fix breakfast.

She set her plate of scrambled eggs and mug of coffee on the dining room table and stepped outside to retrieve the newspaper. Her neighbor, Mrs. Feldstein across the street, was sitting on a bench outside her home, sipping from a coffee mug while her toddler grandson sat beside her, playing with his toy truck.

"Good morning, Mrs. Feldstein. You're up early."

"Tommy slept over." She gave the boy a

sideways glance. "Woke me up before sunrise."

Isabel chuckled. "Good luck."

Between sips of coffee and forkfuls of scrambled eggs, she perused the Philadelphia Inquirer. The first headline in the food section gave her an adrenaline rush. *Famous Restaurateur to Open New Eatery Downtown.*

Her eyes narrowed and her cheeks warmed. Of all the places to open another restaurant, Chris Mackenzie had to choose Philadelphia. She was filled with an array of emotions: anger that tightened her chest, regret that stuck in her throat, a little sadness that tore at her heartstrings, but what scared her the most was the tiny sliver of joy that loosed butterflies in her tummy.

***

Later that morning, Isabel rushed through the glass entryway of the building that housed her employer, *Fit Cuisine Magazine.* Her morning coffee had kicked up her energy level, and she was excited to get back to work on the article she'd been writing.

Cold Sweat

She set her purse on her desk, sat in her comfy computer chair, and inhaled the scent of her apple cinnamon potpourri. Next to the fragrant bowl stood a photo of her at eight years old, sandwiched between her parents on a crowded beach one 4th of July. "Good morning, Mom and Dad."

She wiggled her fingers over the keyboard, and then opened the document file for her latest article: *Recipes to Please Picky Eaters*. Less than five minutes after settling in, she received an email from her boss, Stan.

"Need to speak with you. Come to my office ASAP."

She sighed and saved her work. *What does he want this time?*

It was a short walk across the newsroom to his glass-encased office in the corner. His secretary, Nancy, greeted her. "Good morning, Isabel. You can go right in."

When she walked through the doorway, she saw Stan typing on his keyboard.

"Ms. Kingston, hang on a sec," he said without looking up.

She took a seat on a plush leather couch. Her eyes darted to a picture on

Stan's desk, a portrait studio shot of him with his wife of thirty years and their two sons. Stan wore the same proud smile twenty years ago that he usually showed at work, and even twenty years ago he had little to no hair.

Diagonal from Stan's desk, stood a large bookcase. Its shelves showcased his bowling trophies and a half dozen of Stan's writing awards: transparent globes, gold cups, and silver vases.

He looked away from his computer, jotted a note on a yellow notepad, and then shifted his focus to her. "Sorry to make you wait."

She stood from the couch and took a seat in front of Stan's desk. "What's so important that you couldn't have just emailed me?"

He leaned back in his chair. "That was a great article you did on diabetes. How's your next one coming along?"

"I'll have a draft to you in a couple of hours." She leaned forward. "You didn't call me in here for small talk. What's really on your mind?"

He smiled. "You caught me. Are you

familiar with the restaurant owner Chris Mackenzie?"

Her heart jumped. "Yeah. Why?"

"He's opening a restaurant downtown, and I'd like to feature a profile on him. Are you up for the story?"

"No way. Chris and I have history. I'm not the best person for that assignment."

He chuckled. "Isabel, I know you. History or no history, your reputation for professionalism speaks for itself. I have no concerns."

"Stan, come on. Things ended badly between us. Assign someone else. How about Shelly or Lauren?"

"Amateurs." He shook his head. "You're my senior writer. I want you on this assignment."

She sighed. "I'd rather die."

"Interview him and attend the grand opening on Friday. Die on Saturday."

A lump formed in her throat. "This Friday?"

"That's not a problem, right?"

"I already have plans for Friday."

"Cancel them."

"I can't."

He furrowed his brow. "What's more important than your job?"

"My dad."

His eyes softened. "Oh, that's right. The anniversary of his death."

"His murder, you mean." She sniffled. "I visit him at the cemetery every year on this date."

"I sympathize with your predicament, but I can't and won't give the biggest event in this city since the Liberty Bell to amateurs. Attend the opening. Visit your dad afterwards. He's not going anywhere."

Stan was right, of course. Her dad had been dead for seven years. She'd visit him at least once a month, sometimes twice, but she wasn't keen on going to the cemetery after dark. "Okay. If you insist."

Stan handed her a folded piece of paper. "Here's the phone number for the restaurant. Make an appointment to interview Mr. Mackenzie." He returned his attention to the computer.

She took that as her cue to get on it.

***

Back at her desk, she unfolded the

paper. *Mackenzie's Eatery.* She dialed the number before her stomach could revolt.

"Mackenzie's."

"Hello. I'm Isabel Kingston from Fit Cuisine Magazine. I need to know when he's free for an interview."

"Let me check his schedule. Please hold."

As she waited for the receptionist to come back on the line, she remembered the last time she saw Chris. Tears had streamed from her eyes as she watched him peel off in his big red truck.

How am I going to get through this interview without making a scene?

Just the thought of seeing him made her palms sweat. She wondered if those feelings for him would return, the desire, the adoration, the love, or would she feel the urge to slap his face and say all the things she wished she'd said back then? *"You lousy, no good for nothing, selfish—"*

"Thank you for holding, Ms. Kingston. Mr. Mackenzie can meet with you tomorrow morning at nine. Will that work for you?"

She'd rather have a tooth pulled. "That's perfect, thank you."

"See you then."

She hung up.

This is going to be a disaster.

She bound her long brown tresses into a messy ponytail and began to put the finishing touches on her article. Last week, she'd reached out to readers through the magazine's website forum, and several moms responded by offering recipes they'd created for their own picky eaters.

One mom, Donna from Chicago, sent a recipe for sweet potato pancakes with a pinch of cinnamon. Another mom, Lydia from Pittsburgh, snuck carrots into her chocolate chip muffins. The recipe that appealed most to her was one for veggie filled mac and cheese, sent by Cassie from Denver.

It only took an hour to make the proper additions and edits, which she knew Stan would revise to his own liking. Such was the symbiotic relationship between writer and editor. After sending him the article, she leaned back in her chair and closed her eyes, more to delay her next project than to relieve any residual fatigue.

Get a grip, girl. Remember what dad

said. "When life serves you lemons, make lemonade."

She selected a pen from her desk organizer and pulled a yellow legal tablet from a drawer to jot down a few questions for tomorrow's interview. *Did you ever love me? Why did you leave me? Do you even care that you broke my heart? Why come back now?* She pressed hard on the pen, causing the paper to rip.

Damn you, Chris.

She ripped the page off the tablet, wadded it up, and tossed it into the trash, along with her broken heart. Her hands shook, and tears dripped down her cheeks. Fighting to take a deep breath and ward off the hurt spilling from her eyes, she dabbed her tears with a tissue then held it crumpled to her runny nose.

This isn't working. I have to find more suitable questions to ask him.

She wondered what the internet had to say about this heartbreaker, opened her browser and typed *Chris Mackenzie* in the search menu. The first result that popped up was a picture of Chris from the back cover of his latest cookbook. He looked just as handsome as she remembered: full, dark brown hair, deep brown eyes, and a smile that immediately drew her in.

In the past six years since their breakup, he had written and published two cookbooks and opened three successful restaurants in Ohio, Delaware, and Manhattan, where he was dubbed *Most Eligible Bachelor* in the New York Post.

As angry as she was at him for leaving her behind, a small part of her felt proud of him for making his dreams come true.

Well done, Chris.

Greg Pearson peeked over the top of her cubicle wall. "Ready for lunch?"

"It's that time already?"

"Yep."

She'd lost herself in taking notes and composing questions for tomorrow's interview. The morning had slipped away. After closing out her browser, she grabbed her purse and looped the leather strap over her shoulder. "Where to?"

"Is Josie's Lunch Spot alright?"

"Sounds delicious." She hooked her arm around his elbow and snuggled up close.

He led her past Stan's office on the way

out. He was leaning against the door frame. When their eyes met, he frowned. It wasn't a look of anger, more like worry. Stan had been a father figure to her since she started working at the magazine, the kind of man she could go to if something was on her mind. He didn't know that, of course. To him, he was just her grumpy old boss.

She smiled at him and mouthed the words, *I got this.* Whether she did or not remained to be seen.

***

Josie's was busy as usual. Their menu had a lot of great sandwiches, but the number one item was the Philly Cheese Steak grinder. The minute she walked in, Isabel could smell the peppers and onions. "I'll have the PCS Grinder," she told the sandwich guy. Greg ordered a Club Deluxe.

He led her to a table by the front window and pulled out a chair for her. "How's this?"

"Fine." She sat down and dug into her lunch. It didn't take long for her to notice that Greg hadn't touched his sandwich. He was staring at her with dark blue eyes she could drown in. His brows were pushed close together like something smelled bad.

"What's wrong? Do I have cheese on my face?" She drew a napkin across her mouth.

He shifted forward in his seat. "No, it's just...you haven't been your cheery self today. Didn't even come by my desk to say good morning."

"I didn't sleep well, is all." Her nightmares were no fun to sleep with.

"Nah. It's more than that. I saw you walk out of Stan's office, white as a sheet. What's going on?"

"Eat your sandwich."

He picked up his Club Deluxe. "So, what can I bring tomorrow night?"

"Nothing. I'm taking care of dinner, and Liv is on dessert duty."

"I don't want to come empty handed. How about wine?"

She set down her grinder and reached across the table to touch his arm. "Are you nervous about meeting Liv?"

He swallowed. "She's the closest thing you have to a sister. I want to make a good impression."

"Sounds fair enough. Her favorite wine is Merlot." She leaned in and pecked him on the cheek. "And don't worry. I'll make sure she keeps her gun holstered and her handcuffs in the car."

He set his sandwich on the wrapper as if he'd suddenly lost his appetite.

She laughed. "Sorry. I couldn't resist."

Chapter 2

By the end of the day, Isabel wanted nothing more than to go home, eat dinner, and veg-out on the couch until it was time to go to bed. However, all those luxuries would have to wait. She had to see the doctor first.

As she drove to her therapy session, she hummed along to the song playing on the radio. The country station always mellowed her out. When she arrived, the parking lot was nearly empty. She took a deep breath before stepping out of the car. These sessions could be brutal, but today's was sure to be tougher than most.

Thank you Chris Mackenzie.

His name was sure to come up.

She walked inside and placed her purse on top of the check-in counter. "Hello again."

"Ms. Kingston. How are you?"

"Tired."

"Have a seat. Doctor Anderson will be

with you soon."

One other person sat in the waiting area, an older gentleman. His left leg was bouncing rapidly as he rocked back and forth. He looked to be a basket-case.

Did he lose someone he loved, too?

Her heart went out to him. Taking her purse, she made her way to the magazine rack, picked out a *People* Magazine, and claimed a chair across from the old guy. She was reading an article about Brad Pit and Angelina Jolie when Dr. Anderson opened her office door.

"Come on in, Isabel."

She set the magazine on the end table and stood. "He was here before me." She indicated the old man. "Shouldn't he go first?"

"Oh. That's Mr. DeKyper, the janitor. He's on break."

"And I thought my job was rough."

Dr. Anderson ushered her into the office and closed the door. "So, how have you been since our last session together?"

Settling on the plush green sofa, she forced a smile. "Great...for the most part." She always started off with a lie, which would soon be unraveled.

Dr. Anderson sat in her black leather chair and crossed her legs at the knees. "I sense some hesitation." By now, her notebook was open and set on her lap, but she'd left her pen wedged behind her right ear. "What's going on?" She adjusted her black-framed glasses, which paired nicely with her short silver hair and light pink lipstick.

Isabel's stomach tightened. "The nightmares are back. It's been over a year without them."

"That's not surprising. A lot of people who have suffered a traumatic event have reoccurring nightmares."

"It's been seven years. I thought these nightmares would be gone by now, permanently."

"Grief doesn't have a time table. The anniversary of your father's death is Friday."

"Murder. He was murdered." Her heartbeat ticked up from a shot of adrenaline. "Seventh anniversary, doctor. And the killer is still out there. I'm sick of not knowing who took my dad from me."

"Take a breath, Isabel. Walk me

through the nightmares."

Isabel wanted to forget them forever, not rehash them with Dr. Anderson. "Do I have to?"

"It'll help. Trust me."

She sighed. "Okay...they start off the same. My dad is working at the firehouse. He and the guys are playing cards, got the late-night munchies, so he volunteers to get snacks from the corner convenience store."

"That's pretty much what happened, right?"

"Except this time, we're not talking on the phone. I'm with him when it happens. Some punk jumps him, stabs him five times, and then takes off with the cash from his wallet." Isabel fought back tears. "I'm standing right there but I can't see the killer's face, just my dad dropping to the ground, cookies, crackers, and candy bars scattered around him. The wallet bounces off his shoulder and lands on top of the torn open grocery bag while the thug is running away. I fall to my knees and cradle his head. He's gasping terribly, and blood is pumping from his neck. My hand is pressed to the wound, but I'm unable to stop the flow. He's whispering to me. I can't make out what he's trying to tell me. "Dad. Dad," I'm crying out. "What did you say? What did you say?" But his eyes are a blank stare. My hands, my clothes, I'm soaked in his blood. I'm screaming and I wake up in a cold sweat."

Dr. Anderson cast her a sympathetic eye, reached for the tissue box on the side table, and offered it to Isabel. "What do you think it means?" Her tone was soft.

Isabel plucked a tissue from the box, sniffled and wiped the tears from her eyes. "It's like his spirit is trying to tell me something I need to know. Is that possible?"

She removed the pen from behind her ear and jotted something in the notebook. "Do you think it's possible?"

"I want it to be...but...I don't know."

"Certain dreams or nightmares carry significance, but I doubt there's a message from the grave in them. The man who murdered your father was never caught. Maybe it's your subconscious telling you not to give up."

"No evidence. No leads. The case has gone cold. There's no hope for justice."

"Perhaps your detective friend can reopen the case."

"Liv is a brilliant detective, but she can't pull a suspect out of a hat."

"I understand, but if I were you, I'd ask her to try."

"Maybe I will."

"How have you been otherwise? You and Greg doing alright?"

Isabel nodded. "Really good, but..."

"But what?"

"I like Greg a lot. We've known each other for a year and have been dating for the past two months, but I can't open up to him about my nightmares."

"Why do you think that is?"

She let out a deep sigh. "The last time I opened my heart to someone, it got shattered, crushed, ripped from my chest, stomped on and destroyed. Do you blame me?"

"You're talking about Chris?"

"At one point we saw a future together. Marriage, kids, white picket fence...everything. Then, just like that..." She snapped her fingers. "He was gone."

"So you're scared."

"Terrified."

"You need to remember something. All relationships carry the potential risk of heartbreak."

"Comes with the territory. I get it. But every time I bring up my dad's murder, Greg doesn't want me to talk about it. It's self defeating he says, like I'm torturing myself to no good end. I quit trying to open up to him."

"You need to decide whether Greg is worth the risk."

"I'm keeping him at arm's length." She twirled a strand of hair around her finger. "Another big problem is that my boss has assigned me to interview Chris and attend his restaurant's grand opening. I'm not happy about the assignment. Greg noticed my change of mood and asked me about it at lunch, but I don't dare tell him Chris is back in the picture, even temporarily. He'll just tell me that will come to no good end, as well."

"How does that make you feel?"

"Alone."

"I see."

"The only way out of this is to quit my

job."

"I can't tell you that the interview won't be awkward or that old feelings won't come up, but once you complete the assignment, you'll have no reason to see Chris again, unless you want to."

"I don't." She crossed her arms.

Dr. Anderson arched her eyebrows. "Are you sure? That was a quick response."

"I don't want him back in my life...I can't—"

"Risk it. I understand. He put you through a lot. Just stay true to yourself."

"It's not easy being pulled in different directions."

"You're a lot stronger than you give yourself credit for, and you've made progress since our first meeting."

She grimaced. "Then why does my heart still hurt so bad?"

"Pain and progress are not the same problem." Her pen went back behind her ear.

It was true. Isabel began these sessions a few months after her dad died. Between dealing with her own grief and helping her mother cope with her spiraling depression, she had found herself in a bad place, emotionally. She'd tried to hold it together but often broke down in tears for no apparent reason. She had to force herself to go places with Liv and Chris, and she often plastered on a smile, so as not to worry them, but inside she was screaming.

Once she started seeing Dr. Anderson, her life took a turn for the better...until Chris left. She'd burst into tears anytime she saw a happy couple holding hands. Panic attacks plagued her when confronted with stressful situations. Now this, seeing the man who'd left her with devastating emotional scars loomed on the horizon. Tomorrow.

Chapter 3

The wind tousled Isabel's hair as she stood outside Mackenzie's Eatery. The old warehouse on Smith Road must've cost a fortune to renovate in the style of an Alpine villa. She'd spent almost an hour trying on outfits to find one that said, *"I'm a professional,"* but also, *"Eat your heart out, buster."* She finally decided on a red tie-waist top with white capri pants and black sandals.

It's just an interview. Ask questions, snap pictures, and leave. Simple.

She squeezed the strap of her satchel and took a deep breath before walking through the chestnut French doorway, head held high and back straight and proud.

Chris, wearing a blue button down shirt with black slacks, stood by the hostess stand and smiled when he saw her walk up. "Good to see you, Bel."

He stepped in for a hug, but she

stopped him with the palm of her hand to his chest. "Let's keep this strictly business."

"Okay. We can do the interview over here." He motioned toward a corner booth by a window.

She took a seat and pulled her list of questions from her satchel, along with a new pen, as not to risk running out of ink. "You've accomplished a lot since the last time I saw you."

Chris chuckled as he sat across from her. "You know me. I always have to stay busy."

"I'm curious, though. Your plate is already full with your restaurants in Ohio, Delaware, and Manhattan, not to mention two cookbooks. Why add to your workload with a new restaurant here in Philly?"

"You're right. I've accomplished my goal, but my aspirations came at a price." He lowered his eyes somberly. "I rarely have time for my friends, and I only see my family a few times a year." He looked up at her, straight in the eyes, as if to drive his next point directly into her brain. "I need that part of my life back, so that's why I decided to open this restaurant close to home."

She felt the muscles in her neck tense up.

"You're back for good?"

"I just moved into a new place two weeks ago."

"Seriously?" Her tone was harsh and she dropped her pen on the floor, along with her jaw, it seemed.

He bent down to retrieve it for her. "That's a better reaction than I thought I'd get."

"I'm sorry." She grabbed the pen from his hand, quickly and carefully as not to make skin-to-skin contact. "That was unprofessional."

"Don't be. I deserved it."

She scowled. "You're right."

"At least my folks are happy I'm back."

She always liked Chris's parents. Mark and Eileen were just as successful and charming as their son. Mark owned a car repair shop, and she was a manager at a PR firm. However, as with most breakups, when the relationship ended with the guy, it also ended with his parents.

Back to the restaurant.

"My readers want to know...what's on

the menu?"

He smiled wide at the opportunity to talk about food. "We have a little bit of everything. For Italian lovers, there's fettuccine Alfredo, margarita flatbread pizza, and pesto gnocchi. For steak enthusiasts, we offer steak tacos in flour tortillas with a rice and bean medley, filet mignon, and steak tips, both served with two sides and drizzled with mushroom sauce.

"That sounds delicious."

"My own recipes. We also created a few chicken entrees and seafood dishes. I've included two items from my cookbooks, cheeseburger sliders with my signature sauce and sweet potato fries, and my cookie crumble chocolate cake. The other desserts are in the hands of my head chef. In fact, his strawberry cheesecake is out of this world."

"Sounds like you've gone all-out. Will you be making frequent trips to check on your other restaurants?"

"I'll video chat with the managers regularly, and I'll visit the restaurants every other month, or so. My phone is always on for any issues that come up."

"What about future plans? Another book perhaps?"

"It's possible, but I really want to start a family."

"You have to get married first. Any contenders?"

Why did I just say that? Rewind. Rewind.

He gave her a sideways glance. "I haven't met the right woman, but I haven't given up hope, either."

She bit the inside of her lower lip, almost to the point of drawing blood. *The right woman?* Did he never move on from her? Or was she not *the right woman* for him, either?

She forced herself to look down at her list. "I have all I need for the article. How about a picture to go with it?" She folded the paper, slid it into her satchel, and removed her Nikon DSLR. "Let's go outside...under the marquee."

"That'll be great." He led the way out.

"Stand there." She pointed to a spot on the ground beneath the lighted sign: *Mackenzie's Eatery.*

"Yes, ma'am."

Looking into the viewfinder, she was taken aback by how sexy she still found his smile. His lips were thin and inviting. When he smiled, she couldn't help but smile back at him. It would only take one shot to get the perfect picture. She wanted to take a dozen more. After the shutter clicked, she felt the need to run before she fell into his arms. She stepped back and placed the Nikon in her bag. "That about wraps things up. I'll be back Friday for the grand opening." She fumbled for her car keys, hoping she'd die before Friday.

"It was really good to see you, Bel."

"Don't work too hard." Her tone was as light and swift as her footsteps to her car.

Get a grip, girl. He broke your heart. Never forget.

***

Back at work, Isabel was still reeling from her interview with Chris. Just the image of him standing beneath the marquee gave her butterflies.

Stop this. You're taken.

A few minutes into writing her profile on Chris Mackenzie, Greg stepped up to the side wall of her cubicle. "I heard you got the Chris Mackenzie assignment."

"Lucky me."

"You sound happy about it."

"I'm being facetious. I'd rather chew glass."

"What's the problem?"

"It's a long story."

"I'm on a break." He smiled slyly.

She wanted to be honest with Greg, but telling him about Chris could sever their relationship. However, secrets had a way of coming out. She took a deep breath, then: "We have history, that's all."

"Oh?" His smile was replaced with a worried frown. "Was it serious?"

"Evidently not. I'm still single."

He scowled. "You know what I mean."

"We dated from high school to college, but after graduation, he got a job offer at a restaurant in Ohio. He accepted it, moved away, and never looked back. Eventually he bought it from the owner and opened two more restaurants."

"He sounds like a decent guy."

"The breakup was painful."

"I'm a little nervous to ask...but do you

still have feelings for him?"

Her heart began to pound. She stood and wrapped her arms around Greg's neck. "I'd be lying if I said he didn't still have a place in my heart. Chris was my first love, but he's in my rearview mirror." She ran her fingers through Greg's wavy blond locks. "You are the one I want to be with."

He exhaled a loud sigh. "You're not kicking me to the curb, then?"

"Not yet," she teased. "I'll see you tonight."

"Dinner. Right."

"And you get to meet Liv."

"Wine. Merlot. Got it."

She gave him a peck on the lips. "Now let me get back to work." She watched him walk away, down the row of cubicles. It was true, what she'd said. Chris was a ghost from her past, and after the restaurant opening article was finished, he'd be out of her life again, for better or worse.

Why couldn't he have just stayed away?

Chapter 4

After she got home from work, Isabel headed straight for the fridge and pulled out the ingredients she needed for the meatloaf: ground beef, eggs, ketchup. On the counter she added to the list: salt, pepper, and bread crumbs. When it came to stretching a pound of hamburger, she was Queen of the Pantry.

As she prepped the dish, she thought about her earlier conversation with Greg and how worried he looked when she told him about Chris. Maybe even a touch hurt. She hated putting him through that, but his humorous attitude afterwards made her realize how much Greg meant to her. She needed to do a better job of showing him how she felt.

She had just placed the meatloaf in the oven when Liv arrived with an aromatic homemade apple pie. "Smells yummy."

"I made it from scratch." She handed

the pie to Isabel.

"You shouldn't have." She caught a whiff of Liv's vanilla-scented body spray.

"You'll be glad I did." She placed her keys in the pocket of her brown jacket, and then hung it on a coat hook in the hallway.

"When do you have time to cook, being a homicide detective and all?"

"I manage." She smoothed her green t-shirt then sat at the dining room table. "When will Greg be here?"

"Any minute. Promise me you won't go all detective on him."

Liv arched an eyebrow. "What's that supposed to mean?" She fluffed her shoulder length blond curls.

"Come on, Liv. You know you can be overprotective at times."

"I don't want to see you get hurt again."

Isabel sighed. "Heartache comes with the territory. It's the risk we take for love. That's what my therapist says, anyway. It's the risk we take when we care about someone."

As frustrating as Olivia Morris could be at times, Isabel was grateful to have her as a friend. They'd met in study hall during their freshman year of high school and connected instantly. Liv was as fiery and vocal as they came, while Isabel was soft-spoken and prone to being a push-over. The two of them brought out the best in each other.

She got down plates from the cupboard, suitable for a casual meal, and utensils and water glasses, then placed them on the table. "Make yourself useful."

As Liv set the table for three: "You really like Greg, huh?"

"He's charming and funny, not to mention good looking." Isabel smiled. "And he's dedicated to his job, but it's not his number-one priority."

"Unlike Chris?"

"I didn't say that."

"You didn't have to." Liv smirked.

"Chris had dreams of owning a restaurant. Now he's dust in the wind. His loss. Now Greg is my man, so don't scare him off."

"I promise, Bel, I'll be on my very best behavior."

"Good. And one more thing." She peeked into the oven to check on the meatloaf. "Can you reopen my dad's murder case? I've been thinking about him a lot lately and I—"

"Bel..." Liv walked into the kitchen and put her hand on Isabel's shoulder. "You don't need to explain yourself to me."

"Then you'll do it?"

"I don't think it's a good idea."

"Why not?"

"The case has been closed for five years. They never found any solid leads."

"But they weren't you."

Liv smiled. "I appreciate your confidence, Bel, but it's not up to me. There's a cold case division for that, and solving this case would be nearly impossible."

"But a little possible, right?" She placed her hands together. "Liv, please. I've got to know who killed my dad. He deserves justice. At least try."

Liv inhaled then exhaled slowly. "Okay, I'll look into it, but it's been seven years. Leads dry up. Memories fade. I'm not making any promises."

She grinned. "I know. I know. But I have a good feeling about it this time." She didn't really, but she was trying to be optimistic. Maybe in her dreams her dad was telling her to never give up.

Liv's phone chimed from inside her jacket pocket. When she retrieved the phone and read the incoming text, she smiled and her cheeks turned rosy. Obviously she wasn't being called into work. That would suck.

"So...who is it?"

Liv looked up from her phone. "Jack Miller."

"Your old partner? What's up with him?"

"He moved back to town a few months ago. Last week, he reached out to me."

Isabel always thought the two liked each other, but since they worked together, neither one had acted on their feelings. "What did he say?"

"He asked if I was busy tonight. I texted back 'yes'."

"Are you going to go out with him?"

"Do you think I should?" Her voice was all breathy.

"I'm not Ann Landers. Don't ask me."

"We were good friends, but if we date and it doesn't work out, what am I left with?

A broken heart like yours?"

"You don't sound like my fearless best friend."

She waved her off. "Me? Fearless? Come on, Bel."

"No. Really. I think you two would make a great couple. Maybe you should take a chance."

She looked down at her phone and smiled as she responded to the text.

"What did you tell him?"

"Call me later."

"Now that's the Liv I know."

As they high-fived each other, the doorbell rang.

Isabel took a deep breath, rushed to the door, and opened it to see Greg. He was looking handsome as always. In a black button down shirt and khaki pants, he was dressed to impress.

"Hey, beautiful." He wrapped his arm around Isabel's waist and brought her close to him, while holding a bottle of wine with his other hand. He gave her a sweet kiss on the lips.

"I hope you have more of that for later." She winked and took the bottle from him.

Liv slid the phone in her pocket. "So this is Greg, huh?" She looked him up and down and smiled slyly. "Not bad."

"Hands off, girlfriend." Isabel hoped Liv would stay true to her word. "Greg. This is my best friend, Detective Olivia Morris. Her friends call her Liv."

"Liv, it is, then, I hope." He offered his hand. "Isabel's told me a lot about you."

She accepted his handshake. "Don't believe any of it. I haven't seen Bel this happy in a long time."

He poured on the charm. "I hope that's my fault."

Isabel guided them to the table, then headed for the kitchen to prepare a salad.

"So, Greg," Liv said loud enough to be heard in the kitchen. "Bel tells me you moved to Philly from Boston."

"Yeah. A year ago, when I landed the job at *Fit Cuisine*."

As she was assembling the salad, she thought back to the first day she and Greg met. She and her co-worker, Maggie, were eating in the cafeteria when Greg walked in with a couple of their co-workers. The women were all giddy and hanging on his every word. She knew his type: charismatic, well spoken, handsome. She knew to stay away from him.

The flirty trio had chosen a table directly across from her and Maggie, and though she could feel Greg's eyes on her, she refused to make eye contact with him. She wanted to finish eating and get the hell out of there quick.

However, as she and Maggie were leaving, Greg rushed toward them. "Hey." He smiled at Isabel and walked alongside her. "I've seen you around but we haven't had the pleasure of meeting. I'm Greg." He put his hand out.

Maggie stopped their forward momentum, grabbed his hand, and gave it a shake. "I'm Maggie."

"And you?" he asked Isabel.

She reluctantly accepted his gesture. "Isabel."

Maggie touched Isabel's arm. "I'll see you later." She looked from Isabel to Greg then back again and mouthed, *"He's cute,"* then rushed out.

"Does that usually work for you?" Isabel asked him.

"What?"

"Flashing that smile and saying an obviously over-rehearsed pick-up line."

He lost his smile. "Ouch. Are you usually this judgmental?"

"I know a player when I see one."

He smiled again. "How about you get to know me before you judge me?"

"Why would I do that?"

"Come on. It'll be fun."

"I'm already having fun."

"You ain't seen nothin' yet."

That was the beginning of his cat and mouse courtship, and as if possessed by the devil, he didn't give up. Isabel had done her best to keep him at arm's length, but after eight months, she caved and went out with him. Dinner and a show. The more time she spent with him, the more comfortable she felt in his presence. It wasn't long before she finally decided to release him from the *friend zone*.

Salad tossed, she carried the bowl into the dining room.

Liv asked Greg, "Where did you work before Fit Cuisine?"

"I was a staff writer for *Must Know*, a

small magazine in Boston. Landed it right after college."

Liv's eyebrows arched. "I went to college in Boston, too. Where did you go?"

"North Eastern. I was on the wrestling team."

That got Isabel's attention. Liv's college boyfriend was on the wrestling team. Something in common for them to talk about while she checked on the meatloaf.

"No kidding. My ex wrestled there. I never missed a match." Liv tapped her foot on the hardwood floor. "Did you letter?"

"I didn't say I was a good wrestler." He laughed.

Isabel looked over her shoulder to see Liv frowning at Greg, as if waiting for him to crack under pressure and reveal some dark secret. So much for not interrogating him, but though he was holding his own, she had to intervene. "Alright, guys. Table the conversation while we eat." She carried the meatloaf to the table and set it in the middle.

***

After dinner, they retreated to the living

room, where Isabel made sure to keep the conversation light. They talked about the latest Marvel movie for a half hour.

"Anyone hungry for dessert?" She gestured to the pie on the counter.

Liv stood. "I should go, but you guys enjoy the pie." She grabbed her jacket off the coat hook. "See you for lunch tomorrow?"

"I'll be there with bells on."

"Oh, before I forget..." She snapped her fingers. "Make a list of anyone your dad may have had problems with. Maybe a name will pop up that's not in the case file. And if you think of anything unusual that happened in the days leading up to his murder, make a note of that too. Maybe I can get the cold case boys interested in what you come up with."

Isabel walked her out. "I'll bring it with me tomorrow."

"Perfect. See you at lunch."

She closed the door then walked to the kitchen and pulled two small plates from the cabinet.

"What was that all about?" Greg called from the living room.

"Liv is looking into my dad's case." She cut and dished out the pie.

"Is that why you've been on edge all day?"

She sighed. "Yeah. The anniversary of my dad's death is Friday." She walked into the living room with the pie. "The police gave up trying to solve his murder, but Liv's going to get the cold case people on it."

He took a bite of pie. "Wow. It's delicious."

"Liv baked it."

"Girl with multiple talents."

"Hey, remember who your girlfriend is." She nudged his leg.

"I haven't forgotten...yet," he teased. "But joking aside, it's not a good idea to reopen the case."

"Why not?"

"You shouldn't test yourself."

"You think I'll break down?"

He took a deep breath. "I get where you're coming from. I wake up every day, missing my mom and wishing I could bring her back."

"It's not the same thing. Your mom was sick. You had time to prepare yourself for her death, to say goodbye."

Greg's mom had been diagnosed with stage-four breast cancer when he was seventeen years old. While he was studying for the SATs, he and his dad took turns caring for her. That was the first thing Greg had shared with her, right before they started dating. It was then that she felt an emotional connection with him.

"I wasn't able to say goodbye to my dad. I need justice for him, and Liv is the best chance I have to get it." She cupped a gentle hand on Greg's cheek. "No matter what happens. I can handle it."

"I don't want to see you disappointed, is all." He set aside his empty pie plate.

Isabel took a deep breath. "I usually go alone, but would you come with me to the cemetery Friday night?"

"I can't. I'm going to my weekly poker night."

"Oh? I thought that was on Thursdays."

"Normally, but I can come by here afterwards, if that's okay?"

"And what do you want to do when you get here?" She leaned in for a kiss.

He pulled her into his lap and kissed her

hard, breathily, like he really meant it. His tongue tasted like apple pie.

When she finally came up for air: "I think we've done enough talking for tonight," she whispered and planted butterfly kisses on his earlobe then nibbled it playfully. "What do you say?"

He dove in for another kiss, their passion growing with every second that passed.

"I take that as a yes." She moved her lips from his mouth to his chin then down to his neck where she inhaled his cologne as if it were some kind of drug. "I want you so bad."

He slipped a hand under the back of her blouse. Nimble fingers found the clasp on her bra and unhooked it with one quick pinch. Now he had unabated access to her back and caressed her skin with his warm hand, gently, compared to how hard she was kissing him. The fires were lit and the flames were growing.

She moaned a little then pulled away. "Come on." She could barely breathe as she took his hand and led the way to her bedroom down the hall.

Cold Sweat

Clothes went flying left and right. This wasn't their first rodeo. She knew what he liked and she rode him hard. It wasn't a sprint to the finish line, it was a marathon, changing positions, changing roles, sideways and upside down. The room spun in lustful bliss, with all the kissing and touching, and sometimes he got a little rough, so she got rough right back at him. Temperatures rose on both ends of the spectrum, high and low, up and down; it was the greatest show on earth.

And the sweet nothings, by God he used them all, you're beautiful, you're hot, your so soft, you smell like rainfall on a cool summer's eve. Lightning and thunder drove her to the abyss and then over the edge she flew, high as a kite and finally coming down, slowly, light as a feather drifting down, down, down until she could finally breathe again, nestled in his arms, so stable, so warm, so safe, so loving. The storm had passed, and nature returned to normal.

Greg had many wonderful qualities, but what she liked most was that he was happy and confident with his position in life. He wasn't looking to make any changes or leave her. She could rest easy knowing that he would never break her heart. With her head on his chest and his arm around her, it was easy to drift into dreamland.

***

Isabel sat up, screaming, drenched in a cold sweat. "Dad. Dad."

Greg woke up, stroked her hair. "You're okay." He spoke in a soothing tone. "It was just a bad dream."

She took a few deep breaths. "My dad...he was talking to me."

"What did he say?"

She shook her head. "His words didn't make sense."

"Dreams seldom do."

"I guess that's true." She glanced at the clock, *10pm*, then placed a hand on his shoulder. "Go back to sleep. I'm going to make myself a cup of warm milk."

"I'll stay up with you." He started to get out of bed, but she put her hand out to stop him.

"You're sweet but I want to be alone."

"You sure?" He laid back down.

"I'll be fine."

After she nuked the milk and sprinkled in a little nutmeg, she sat on the couch and sipped her soothing drink. She'd taken a picture of her and her father down from the bookshelf, and running her thumb over the edge of the silver frame, she studied the photo closely. It was taken in front of the firehouse. She was six years old and standing next to him. He wore his dress uniform. She always thought of him as a handsome, brave prince. He was tall with a muscular build and had short brown hair and blue eyes like hers.

While staring at the photo, she thought about her latest nightmare. She was walking with him when his killer approached them. He was wearing dark clothes and a hoodie. She couldn't make out his face. But this time, as she held her dying father, she heard him speak loud and clear. *"Beware of Ethan."*

Ethan? Who is Ethan?

She couldn't help but wonder if he was speaking to her beyond the grave, warning her of some guy named Ethan. Why would he do that? She wasn't open to a new romance. Maybe somebody at work. A new guy? Ethan made no sense.

She sipped her milk and wondered if Ethan was his killer. Maybe he recognized the punk, maybe that's why he was stabbed to death, so he couldn't tell, get the punk arrested and sent to jail. She should tell Liv...call 9-1-1, get the cold case boys on it, pronto.

Then again and more likely, dreams never made any sense, but she'd rather believe they made perfect sense.

What are you trying to tell me, Dad?

Chapter 5

The next day, Isabel walked into *Penny's Good Luck Charm Diner,* looking for Liv for their lunch date. She was already there, waving her over to a window-facing booth.

The diner was crowded, filled with the din of customers talking and laughing. Walking toward Liv, she caught a whiff of someone's cheeseburger.

Mmm. Bacon.

When Isabel sat across from Liv, she noticed the table was shaking. Liv's right knee was bouncing against a table support. She only did that when she was nervous about something, which was almost never.

A waitress stepped up before Isabel had the chance to ask what was the matter.

"Ladies, welcome to Penny's. What can I get you?"

Isabel knew what she wanted. "I'll have one of your famous BLTs with fries and a lemonade, please."

"I'll have the same." Liv's knee was still bouncing.

The waitress hustled away.

"Liv, what's up? You're nervous as a man in a maternity ward."

"I have a lot on my plate at work."

"Anything to do with my dad's case?"

"I'm working with the cold case team. We have the report submitted by the detective who led the case, as well as a box of evidence collected from that night, the snacks, his wallet, even the torn grocery bag."

"What can you tell me?"

"Nothing. There were no witnesses and the murder weapon was never found. Security footage from outside the market was dark and grainy, couldn't make out the killer's face. He appeared to be taller than your dad, maybe six feet, average build. That's all we know about him."

"Oh." Isabel lowered her head.

The waitress delivered their lemonades.

Liv took a sip of her drink. "According to the medical examiner's notes, the knife he used was single edged and serrated, like any of a million steak knives, so he was no Rambo."

Isabel stared into her lemonade. "It's hopeless."

"Don't worry, Bel. I haven't given up. Do you have that list?"

"Oh, yeah..." She removed the list from her pocket. "I wrote down the names of all the guys my dad worked with, some bowling buddies, and a couple of neighbors." She pointed to one name on the list. "Lou Hunter, here. He had a beef with my father over a misunderstanding. That was a few months before the murder."

"I don't recall seeing his name in the file."

"Lou had confided in my dad that he was in a lot of debt and in jeopardy of losing his house. My dad offered to loan him some money, but Lou was too proud to accept it. He begged my dad not to say anything to anyone, but somehow Lou's wife found out he'd been gambling again. She filed for divorce. Lou accused my dad of telling her."

"Looks like a new lead."

"I can't thank you enough."

"I'm happy to do it. Elliot was like a dad

to me."

Truer words were never spoken. Liv's dad walked out on her and her mom when she was twelve years old. After he left, her mom had to work two jobs and was rarely home. They were never really close, and things became worse as she got older, until finally her mom just up and left, "for greener pastures" as Liv would say.

When she and Isabel became friends, Elliot made it his responsibility to look out for Liv, showing her the same care and concern he did for Isabel.

The irony is that Liv's dad reached out to her shortly after she and Isabel graduated from high school. He gave her a half-assed apology and said he was trying to work out his issues. In her feisty and no nonsense way, Liv told him to shove his apology up his ass, along with his issues. She had found all the family she needed. He never bothered her again.

"Here you go, ladies. Enjoy." Their waitress placed their sandwich orders on the table.

Isabel swallowed a bite of her sandwich. "It just dawned on me. I never told you about my interview with Chris."

"That's because you were too busy making sure I didn't unlawfully arrest your boyfriend."

"Very funny."

"How'd it go?"

"It was awkward at first. He greeted me like no time had passed, like our relationship didn't end with bitterness and resentment."

Liv finished chewing a French fry. "I sense there's a *but* coming."

"After I made it clear that it was strictly business, our meeting got less awkward. He's still dedicated to his work, but get this. He wants to settle down and have a family."

Liv arched an eyebrow. "That's a switch."

"I'm happy for him, but after the grand opening, I'll never see him again."

"That's Friday, right?"

"At six. Then I'm going to visit my dad."

"You have to be realistic, Bel. Chris is living in Philly now. You're bound to run into him sometime. You need to decide how you're going to handle it when that happens."

Liv finished her sandwich then placed her napkin on top of the empty plate. "I'll get the check."

Isabel polished off her lemonade. "Thanks, but we got the same thing. We'll split it."

"Dutch is fine with me." She raised her hand. "Check please."

Bill paid, Isabel followed Liv outside. "What's next?"

Liv stopped to make a phone call. "Hey, Danny. Run the name Lou Hunter for me. Get me everything you can on him and see where he was on the night Elliot Kingston was murdered."

For the first time in years, Isabel felt hopeful that justice for her dad was near at hand. They finally had a solid lead. "Do you think he did it?"

"Lou had motive but did he have opportunity? That's the question now."

"I guess we'll soon find out."

***

Isabel returned to work, a bit lighter on her feet, until she found an email from Stan waiting in her inbox:

Maggie is out sick today. I need you to cover her assignment. Thanks.

Maggie handled quizzes, horoscopes, myths, and Top-10 lists. Today's assignment was on paranormal myths. Writing it would be easier said than done. Her knowledge of the supernatural could fit on a microscope slide.

In Maggie's cubicle, she found Maggie's notebook, a good place to start, but after a quick thumb-through, she saw only a few notes, which didn't offer much to go on.

Ghosts only come out at night; Only old houses are haunted.

She flipped through the notebook again, hoping for any tidbit she could use.

Hold on. What's this?

She'd found a draft of a previous article Maggie had written on dreams.

It can feel spooky when a loved one who's passed over talks to you in your dreams. This experience can be frightening and bewildering, and though such an occurrence has never been proven scientifically, there have been millions of reported accounts of this happening throughout history.

You may wonder: Is your dream real? If you awaken with the feeling of being watched, it's real. If you wake up screaming in a cold sweat. It's real. What should you do if your deceased loved one talks to you in your dreams?

Don't panic.

Listen.

Take notes.

Heed the words you hear.

Be wary of trouble coming.

Her heart flip-flopped. There was no doubt about it. Her dad was reaching out to her, warning of trouble to come. Ethan was the clue, but who was Ethan? Was he a real person? Was he the killer? What trouble would he bring?

Dad. I hear you but I don't understand you.

She closed the notebook and leaned back in her chair. There were so many questions and none with answers. Could be that Lou Hunter was off the hook.

At least I'm not going crazy.

She decided to write an article about ghosts. Everybody believed in ghosts. She went to work.

Once she was finished with Maggie's assignment, she continued to work on Chris's profile. It didn't take her long to finish it.

Restaurateur and former Philadelphia resident, Chris Mackenzie is celebrating his latest success: his new Philadelphia restaurant, Mackenzie's Eatery.

For the past six years, Mackenzie, 28, has been working to make a name for himself in the restaurant industry. The new restaurant will be the fourth in Mackenzie's franchise, the other locations being in Ohio, Delaware, and Manhattan.

Mackenzie is also the proud author of two bestselling cookbooks- Delicious Recipes for Every Level Cook and Mackenzie's How-to Guide for Fine Dining Cuisine.

At this point in his career, Mackenzie has decided to move back to Philadelphia for his latest business venture.

"I've accomplished my goal but my aspirations came at a price," Mackenzie says. "I need family back in my life, so that's why I decided to open this restaurant close to home."

The menu consists mostly of Italian entrees and steak dinners, but Mackenzie said there will also be chicken and seafood dishes available.

"I have included two items from my cookbooks," Mackenzie says. "My cheeseburger sliders with my signature sauce and sweet potato fries, and my cookie crumble chocolate cake."

Although Mackenzie will be living in Philadelphia, he will continue to have an active role in the conduct of his other restaurants.

The grand opening of Mackenzie's Eatery will be held Friday evening at 6 p.m. For information and reservations, visit MackenziesEaterydotcom.

Isabel sat back and sighed. Liv was right. Now that Chris was living in Philadelphia, they would most likely run into each other from time to time. It didn't have to be awkward or emotional.

Hey, how are you? Good, thanks. Goodbye.

It was that simple.

I can do that. I think.

As she signed off on her computer, Greg

came by her cubicle. "Ready for that movie?"

"Yup."

***

Greg led Isabel into the theater early, so they had a wide selection of seats from which to choose. As she scanned the auditorium for the perfect row, she heard a man call her name. The voice was unmistakable. Her throat tightened.

Great, just great.

Chris walked up, carrying a big bag of popcorn. "Fancy meeting you here."

"I didn't know you were into rom-coms," she said as sarcastically as she could.

"My movie tastes have changed a bit over the years." He chuckled. "Who's the lucky man?" He was looking at Greg.

She hooked her arm around Greg's elbow. "Chris, I'd like you to meet my boyfriend, Greg."

Chris held out his hand. "Nice to meet you, man."

"Likewise." Greg shook Chris's hand but pulled it away quickly. She could tell by the way he took a step back that he was uncomfortable being chummy with her ex. "Enjoy the movie," he added flatly.

Chris pointed to the front. "I like to sit up close. Catch you after the show?"

"No." She shook her head. "I'll see you Friday. Come on, Greg." She led him to the middle seats in the middle row.

He abruptly plopped down before she was seated. "So that was Chris, huh?"

"Yeah." She sat next to him. "But like I said, he and I are history."

"Does he know that?"

"Of course."

He huffed. "Seems like he's still interested in you."

"He was just being polite, but if it's too weird for you, we can leave."

"It's fine."

The lights were dimming, but she wanted to make sure he wasn't thinking there was something going on between her and Chris. She leaned in closer. "Are you sure you're fine?" She placed her hand on his arm. "You seem agitated."

He jerked his arm away. "I said I'm fine. Just let it go." He'd raised his voice.

She'd never seen the jealous side of

him before, and she didn’t care for it. However, she didn't want to make a scene in public, so she reclined her seat back and got comfortable for the previews.

She must have gotten too comfortable. It wasn't until Greg gently shook her awake that she realized she'd fallen asleep. She sat upright. "What did I miss?" she asked, a little panicked.

"Let’s get the hell out of here."

Though she was disappointed about missing the movie, that hour and a half was the best sleep she’d gotten in weeks.

Walking to the car, she turned to Greg. His face was stone cold. Jealousy was not a good look on him.

His attitude could be a deal breaker.

***

The car ride home was silent and awkward. Usually when he was driving, he'd give her a side glance and smile. Then he would move his hand to cover the top of hers. Tonight, he kept his eyes on the road and his hands firmly on the steering wheel.

He pulled his car into her driveway, shut it off, and glanced at her with puppy dog eyes. "I'm sorry about earlier."

She crossed her arms and looked away. "You were rude to me."

"I guess my jealousy just got the better of me."

"Guess? You guess?"

"Forgive me?"

"Are you out of your mind?"

"I'm crazy, alright. Crazy about you. Can you give me a break? It won't happen again."

She shot him a sideways glance. After Friday, Chris wouldn't be an issue any longer, so she decided to cut Greg some slack. "Alright. This time. And there better never be a next time."

He leaned in with his lips puckered.

She pushed his face back. "Forget it."

"Then let's go inside."

"I'm going in. You're going home." She jerked the handle and shoved the door open. "See you at work."

"I hope you're not still mad tomorrow."

She slammed the door, stepped back, and watched him peel out of the driveway.

Bet he learned his lesson.

She chuckled. It was fun to make him

grovel. He deserved it.

Inside, after she slipped into her pajamas, her phone rang. It was Liv.

"Hey, Bel, Lou Hunter has a solid alibi for that night. He was bowling and has a dozen corroborators."

"Oh."

"We're back to square one. Sorry, Bel."

"Are you going to keep digging?"

"I need to find a shovel first. Bye for now."

She plugged her phone into the charger, not surprised Lou didn't do it. Her dad would have told her so.

Climbing into bed, she hoped for a deep, uninterrupted sleep. Unfortunately, her movie theater nap was the best rest she'd get. She dreamed of knife-wielding attackers, dripping blood, and dying dads. She tossed and turned. At one point she sat up crying. Her father's words haunted her.

"Beware of Ethan."

Chapter 6

The next morning, Isabel lay flat on her back, staring at her bedroom ceiling. The sun peeked through her curtains, and she heard birds chirping beyond the window, but all she could focus on was her father's dying words as she cradled him in her dreams. They weren't nightmares anymore, but messages from her dad. She wondered if her mother had heard from him, as well.

She unplugged her phone from the charger and scrolled through her contact list until she found *MOM*. As the phone rang, she hoped her mother wouldn't think she was crazy.

The call connected. "Isabel? Are you alright?"

"I know it's last minute, but can I come over?"

"Of course, but...what's the matter? You never call me in the morning."

"Great. I'll see you soon."

"Isabel?"

She ended the call.

Driving toward Mom's house, she decided to stop somewhere first. She pulled to the curb in front of *All You Need Market*. After getting out of the car, she strode to the spot across the street where her father had been killed. To her it was hallowed ground.

She closed her eyes and replayed the events of that night, starting with the phone call she'd made to him. When he answered the phone, she could tell he wasn't inside the fire station. The wind was blowing across his mic, and she heard cars passing by. "Isabel. You should be in bed."

"I'm not a little girl anymore, Dad. It's ten o'clock. Where are you?"

"I volunteered for a snack run."

She heard the bell ring as he entered the store, and by the lack of noise in the background, she assumed the place wasn't busy.

"What are you going to buy?"

"The guys wanted Cheetos, barbeque chips, candy and cookies."

"Yum."

"I got me a pack of them little sugar donuts."

She heard him set the items on the counter. "How are you tonight?" her father asked the clerk.

"Can't complain. And yourself?"

"Long day. Longer night." He chuckled.

Then came the sound of a grocery bag crinkle open and items dropped inside. "That'll be ten forty-two."

"Thanks."

The bell rang again. "I'm heading back now. So why did you call?"

"It's Chris. He's been acting weird lately, quiet, aloof."

"Well, you're both getting ready to graduate. Thinking about the future can be nerve-wracking."

"That's true."

"Honey, I have never seen two people more in love than you and Chris, other than your mother and I, of course. Whatever hurdles come your way, you can overcome them, together."

"Thanks, Dad."

"Please, son. You don't have to do this."

"Dad?"

"Just give me the money," she heard a man say.

"Dad? Dad, can you hear me?"

"I can help you, get you a job. I know a man who owns an auto shop. You don't need that knife."

"Shut up, just shut up," the man screamed. "Gimme your wallet."

"Take it and go."

She heard her dad's phone clatter on the ground, a thud and a painful groan...

The line went dead.

The memory was so vivid, it could have happened yesterday. However, this time a detail jarred her to the core. The wallet. Her dad gave him the wallet, but it was left at the crime scene.

"Why?" she muttered.

***

When Isabel pulled into her mom's driveway, she was standing in the doorway of her light yellow Cape Cod ranch, smiling. Even early in the morning, she was stunning: tall, with wavy honey-blond hair and light green eyes. She was dressed in a teal green blouse, black pants, and sandals. "You have me a little worried, sweetheart. Is everything okay?"

Isabel shook her head. "Not really." Her voice quivered.

Her mother held out her arms for a hug.

Meredith Kingston's big hugs were comparable to a delicious chocolate chip cookie that a mom would give to a crying child after a visit to the doctor. No matter how down Isabel felt, a hug from her mother would always lift her spirits.

Her mother started to let go, but Isabel pulled her back in.

"What's wrong, honey?" She stroked the back of Isabel's head with a soft and soothing touch.

"I'm better now." When she was finally ready to let go, she followed her mother inside.

"Do you want something to drink?"

"No. I'm okay."

They walked into the living room and sat on a black leather couch.

"Where is Bill today?"

"He went home a little while ago."

Bill Henson was her mother's neighbor.

They started dating about two years ago. He was a good guy, retired, tall as the sky with eyes just as blue, and salt and pepper hair. At first it was strange to see her mother with someone who wasn't her father, but over time, she grew to appreciate his presence in their lives. He made her mother smile and laugh in a way that Isabel hadn't seen since her father died.

"You know I'm always happy to see you, honey, but I am a bit curious. Why drive forty minutes out of your way for a hug?"

"I used a personal day off. I need to talk to you about Dad."

"Oh?"

"Those nightmares are back again."

"I'm an expert on nightmares, for sure."

"I need to know, does Dad talk to you in your dreams?"

"Talk to me? What are you saying?"

"Dad's trying to tell me something."

"Isabel. Have you told Dr. Anderson about this?"

"I did but I need to talk to the expert."

After Elliot died, Meredith went through a deep depression. She woke up crying in the middle of the night, was always late for work and barely saw any of her friends or family members.

From her own experience with depression, Isabel knew how beneficial therapy could be. Eventually, Meredith took her advice and began seeing a psychiatrist who helped her realize that she needed a new start. So, she found a job as a library director in West Chester and bought this nice house nearby. She had been doing well ever since.

Meredith pressed on. "Tell me about these nightmares."

"Do you know anyone named Ethan?"

A quizzical expression crossed her face, then: "Not that I recall."

"Did Dad know an Ethan?"

"I don't think so. Where is this coming from?"

"In my dreams, instead of me on the phone with him, I'm cradling him as he dies."

"Oh, honey, that sounds terrifying."

"He whispers to me, *Beware of Ethan*."

Meredith scrunched up her brows. "I don't know what that means."

"I'm going to have Liv look for any

Ethan connected to dad. She's reopened the cold case."

"That was smart. Do you want to stay here tonight?"

"Mom. We're talking about Dad."

"It still hurts, you know that. I don't want to cry..."

"Okay. I'm sorry. What about tonight?"

"We'll order out for dinner, and I'll make you a nice breakfast in the morning."

"That sounds great."

"How about we start with a trip down memory lane?"

"But, Mom. You said you don't want to cry."

"Good memories make me smile." Her mom went down to the basement, then came back up, carrying a box of photo albums.

They spent the next few hours smiling and laughing at all of the funny memories caught on camera. Isabel's favorite was the picture her mom took after her father burnt off his eyebrows while trying to light the grill. He was wearing his corny "Kiss the Cook" apron and holding his spatula like a dagger. That was the only time he didn't smile for a photo.

Isabel laughed so hard, she almost fell off the couch while her mom had a coughing fit.

"I don't know about you, but I'm starving." Meredith took a big gulp of water to calm her cough.

"I could eat a horse, but I don't think we have enough catsup."

"Blah." Mom shuddered.

They decided to have a late lunch/early dinner, a meal of appetizers from a sports bar down the street. Mom ordered boneless wings, mozzarella sticks, and brew-pub pretzels. After eating, they would watch a couple of rom-coms.

DoorDash showed up with their order, and it wasn't long before Isabel was chomping on a mozzarella stick. "I'm glad we did this, Mom."

Meredith nodded as she munched on a boneless wing. "It's wonderful to spend time with you."

Once they finished eating, Isabel fixed them each a cup of hot chocolate while Meredith readied the first of their movies: *Legally Blonde*.

Two movies later, Isabel felt herself dozing off. "I'm going to bed."

"I'm with you." Mom yawned.

Isabel hugged her goodnight. "Thanks for a fun day, Mom."

"My pleasure, honey. Goodnight."

She walked down the hall to the guest room and laughed when she saw a pair of pink flannel pajamas laid out on the bed. "Thanks, Mom," she called out down the hall. The TV was off and the lights were out.

Within seconds of her head hitting the pillow, Isabel's eyelids closed, and soon she was walking arm-in-arm with her father through Benjamin Rush State Park. They were enjoying a calm morning. The wind was gently blowing through her hair, the birds chirped a Snow White melody, and squirrels were running up and around the trunks of red maple trees. She walked with him in complete silence, until her father stopped abruptly and turned to her. "He's close, Isabel."

"Who?"

He fell backwards, and knife wounds suddenly spurted blood.

"Dad. Dad." She awoke in a cold sweat,

screaming.

Meredith ran into the bedroom, turned on the light. "Isabel, honey. What's wrong?" She was out of breath.

"Dad..." She gasped heavily. "He...he came...to me...again," she managed between shuddering sobs.

Her mother rushed to the bed and took her gently by the hand. "It was just a dream. Come on. You're sleeping with me."

She crawled into her mother's bed and snuggled up next to her, but she didn't go back to sleep. She lay there for hours, eyes wide open, thinking about her father's words.

Who is close? Ethan? What are you trying to tell me, Dad?

Chapter 7

The next morning, Isabel awoke in an empty bed. She heard her mother shuffling about in the kitchen, bacon frying and coffee percolating. "Ah, Mom." She got up to go help.

"Did I wake you?" her mother asked, spatula in hand.

"I didn't sleep much. Breakfast smells divine." She examined the fare. "French toast and bacon. My favorite foods."

"I know what my little girl likes." She opened the fridge and took out a carton of orange juice.

Isabel set the table. Meredith delivered the goods then sat in her usual chair. Isabel poured coffee and joined her mom.

Meredith forked a wedge of French toast. "It took you a while to get back to sleep last night."

"Eventually." She took a sip of orange juice. "Thanks for letting me sleep with you."

"Reminded me of when you were little. Thunder did the trick back then, but now...your father talking to you? That's a tough storm to sleep through."

"It's possible, you know. I've read about it happening. Spooky in a way, but I need to listen to him."

"Don't get yourself all worked up over a dream. I hate to see you so frightened."

"I'll be alright."

After breakfast, she cleared the table, and then went to the spare bedroom to get ready for work.

"I'm going, Mom." She stopped at the front door.

Meredith rushed from the kitchen. "Don't be a stranger, dear." She walked Isabel to her car then gave her a tight squeeze. "Have a great day," she whispered softly in her ear.

"Love you, Mom." She started the car and backed out of the driveway. Greg was probably freaked out that she didn't go to work yesterday. She hadn't talked to him since the movie theater incident. Good to let him sweat, but she wasn't sure how eating crow had affected his mood.

She called Liv.

"Bel, what's up?"

"I have a name. Ethan. See if it pops up in the case file anywhere."

"I don't recognize it. Do you have a last name?"

"No."

"But it's a lead...how?"

"Call it a gut feeling."

"I'll see what I can find out."

Ethan has to be involved. I'm on it, Dad.

***

At work, a cup of fresh coffee sat on her desk. A purple sticky note attached to it read: *"See you tonight - G."*

Right. He's coming over after I get back from the cemetery.

But, hey, there was nothing like the comfort of coffee to inspire a writer. By her last sip, she had finished an article on *Healthy Food Tips for Expectant Moms*, and was ready to tackle her next project on the dos and don'ts of exercising. This one was particularly challenging, given that her only form of exercise was walking with Liv to and from *Bagel Palace* every Sunday for breakfast.

She was halfway done with the article, when she decided she needed a break. 11:45 was close enough to lunchtime. She headed downstairs to the cafeteria.

As she was paying for her tuna salad sandwich, she heard Greg call her name. He was sitting at a table in the middle of the room. She joined him for lunch.

"So, tonight's the big night," he said.

"Yeah. The restaurant opening."

"Then you're going to the cemetery?"

"Right. It's not too late to cancel your poker game and come with me." She added a flirtatious smile.

Greg swallowed a bite of his sandwich then wiped mayo off the side of his mouth. "I can't cancel on the guys. They'd think I was pussy-whipped or something."

"Okay. I get it." She shouldn't have brought it up.

He ate his sandwich without so much as looking up at her.

Fine. Be that way.

After rushing through her lunch, she stood.

"Hey, where's the fire?"

"I'm not in the mood for your crap, Greg."

"We're still on for tonight, right?"

"I should be home by nine. If you're over your hissy fit about Chris, I'll see you then. Otherwise, don't bother."

He waved her off and she walked out. She wanted to get back to her desk and write an article about food poisoning. Greg seemed different, colder, less caring. Maybe she'd been too hard on him over his jealousy.

But damn it. After tonight, Chris is out of the picture. What's Greg got to worry about? Nothing.

As soon as she got back to her cubicle, she opened her document and continued working on her article. She proofread it a couple of times before sending it to Stan. Then she walked to his office.

His secretary gave a nod of approval before she entered. "Hey, Stan, I was wondering if I could take off a little early today...like right now. I need to get ready for the restaurant's grand opening."

"Sure. You did a great job on the

Mackenzie profile. I look forward to seeing pictures of the festivities."

"See you Monday."

Chapter 8

When Isabel got home, she kicked off her shoes and headed to her room. She needed to select an outfit that said *Professional* and *Beautiful*. Combing through an array of dresses in her closet, she found the perfect outfit: blue jeans that hugged every curve and a blouse with a subtle V-neckline and a pretty lace pattern on the back. For makeup, she went with a light shade of brown eye-shadow, black eyeliner, and pink lipstick.

Once she was ready to leave, she grabbed her black clutch and red jacket, and then slipped into her matching red heels. One check in the mirror, she was ready for anything. "Eat your heart out, Chris Mackenzie."

The restaurant parking lot was packed. She drove around twice before finally finding a space on the street.

Once she put the car in park, she pulled

her visor down and opened the mirror for a makeup check. Eyeliner and eyeshadow, perfect. Lipstick, smooth and luscious.

Okay, you've got this, girl.

Her legs felt wobbly as she walked toward the entrance. Tonight was the last time she had to mingle with Chris. On the one hand, she was relieved. On the other hand, she wanted more conversations, trips down memory lane, closure to the heartbreak he'd left in his wake.

As she walked in, Chris spotted her immediately. "Bel, hey." His smile was wide and eager. He rushed toward her with a menu under his arm. "I'm happy you could make it. Follow me." He led her to a *Reserved VIP* table across from a young couple. They were smiling at one another while sharing a wedge of strawberry cheesecake.

The restaurant was packed, not a table or booth was left empty. Each table had an electric candle in the center. The booths were spacious with leather upholstery, and floral art pieces hung on every wall. In the center of the restaurant's ceiling hung a crystal chandelier that sparkled with just the right amount of flash.

"Chris, this place looks fantastic."

He rolled back on his heels shyly. "It does, doesn't it." He handed her the menu. "Ellie's going to be your waitress tonight. I'll swing back over as soon as I can."

"Great." She removed her cell phone from her clutch and snapped a few pictures to capture the ambiance around her, then set the phone on the table and picked up the menu. There were so many delicious-sounding entrees. The cranberry balsamic chicken and the lemon garlic salmon made her mouth water, but she knew what she wanted the moment she saw it. Chicken parm. *Yum*.

Ellie stepped up and set a glass of water on the table. "Can I start you off with something to drink?"

"Raspberry lemonade will be fine."

"Good choice. We fresh-squeeze every glass. Do you need a few minutes to look over the menu?"

"My mind is set on the chicken parm, heavy on the parm, please."

"Great choice. We fresh-squeeze our chickens, too."

They laughed.

"I'll put that order in now and be right back with your drink."

Ellie was sweet and funny, made her want to come back to Mackenzie's Eatery. She'd remember that for her review.

"Here you go." Ellie set the lemonade on the table.

"That was fast."

"You get special treatment. Boss's orders."

Chris was either trying to impress her to win her over or plying for a good writeup in Fit Cuisine. She scanned the room and listened carefully. The entire wait staff was delightful. Definitely worth mentioning in the her article on the grand opening.

Ellie walked over, carrying a tray with Isabel's chicken parm on top. "Be careful, the plate is hot." She placed the plate carefully on the table. "Enjoy."

The chicken parm took Isabel back to the first time she had a real conversation with Chris. They were in their sophomore year of high school, both taking the Family & Consumer Science elective course. She had been wanting to talk to him for months but could never muster more than a three word sentence to him.

"Nice day, right?" she said one day while they were waiting for class to begin. The teacher came in before Chris had the chance to respond. Another time, he initiated, *"Hey, how are you?"* She responded, *"Hey, good, thanks."* She was so nervous she walked away before the conversation could pick up.

One day, fate intervened. Their assignment was to create a dish around chicken.

She'd been struggling with C grades all semester, but this time she was going to fail miserably. Her lemon basil chicken was overcooked...well...slightly burned, while her rice pilaf was under seasoned to the point it tasted like balsa-wood. The teacher actually had a coughing fit when she sampled it.

Chris, on the other hand, nailed his chicken parm and veggie noodles. It was beautifully cooked and had just the right amount of flavoring. The teacher was so impressed that she had everyone come up and sample a forkful for themselves.

This was Isabel's opportunity to have a genuine conversation with him. She took a deep breath before walking up to him. "Hey, Chris. I don't want to fail this class. Do you think you could give me a few tips?"

"I would but I have a huge English paper due next week. I have no idea where to start."

"Hmm. Maybe we can help each other out. English is my best subject."

"It's a deal." He offered a handshake to solidify the arrangement.

His grip was strong, and just touching his hand let the butterflies loose in her stomach.

They spent the next week working together, outside of class, until finally, Chris asked her out. Instead of the clichéd dinner and movie date, he took her to a traveling carnival set up outside the local mall.

Isabel loved carnivals but this one stood out. Instead of the basic calliope music playing, there was a live band. She and Chris were close to the stage and sang along to her favorite country song, *All American Girl.* She'd swayed from side to side, sometimes touching elbows with Chris.

He didn't seem to mind.

It was an unforgettable date. Good food, fun rides, games that neither of them won, and best of all, a kiss that was worthy of an A in chemistry.

Chris walked up to her table just as she swallowed her first mouthful of chicken. "Chicken parm and veggie noodles, huh? How is it?"

She dabbed her mouth with a napkin. "Reminds me of a carnival for some reason."

"Hmm..." He tilted his head. "A Carrie Underwood song comes to mind. Does the meal meet your expectations?"

"Deliciously."

"I'm glad to hear it. Be sure to mention that in your article."

"Of course."

So much for trying to win me over.

"For dessert, you should try the strawberry cheesecake. The chef's recipe is top secret. He even refuses to share it with me."

She giggled. "I'd love some, but I can't stay too long. After I finish eating, I need to talk to a few customers and take some pictures. Then I'm heading to the cemetery to visit my dad. It's the anniversary of—"

"I can email you a bunch of pictures. That way you can leave sooner."

"That would be great. Thanks."

"I better make the rounds. I'll send Ellie over with the cheesecake."

She polished off the last of the chicken and veggie noodles. The seasoning was right on point, just as she remembered. The strawberry cheesecake was rich and creamy. Chris had himself a fine restaurant here, and she planned to write a flattering article. Straight As, five stars.

"Here's your check, hon," Ellie said. "It's not fresh-squeezed, I assure you."

"Your service is impeccable." She handed Ellie her expense account card. "Add a fifty dollar tip."

Stan can afford it.

After she signed the credit card slip, she walked around the restaurant and spoke to several customers who all gave a variation of the same response: great food, nice ambiance, super service, and an attentive restaurant owner.

One couple in particular were avid travelers and had been to Chris's other restaurants. They were here celebrating their 10th wedding anniversary. "Mr. Mackenzie's restaurants never disappoint." The wife made sure her anniversary present was on display for Isabel to notice. A beautiful white gold and diamond tennis bracelet.

"Congratulations."

As Isabel was about to leave, she heard a woman call her name. She turned to see Chris's mom standing by a table a few rows down from the front door. She was wearing a pretty white dress adorned with a splash of flowers that brought out her hazel eyes.

"Isabel, honey. It's so good to see you." She wrapped her in a hug, and Isabel caught a whiff of lilac-scented shampoo in her short auburn hair.

"It's good to see you too, Mrs. Mackenzie." She pulled out of the hug to acknowledge Chris's dad, who was sitting on a chair at the other side of the table. "Hi, Mr. Mackenzie."

He smiled. "I think you've known us long enough to call us Eileen and Mark." His voice was deep and thick as maple syrup. He stood and walked closer to Isabel.

"How've you been?"

Mark was a big guy with dark brown hair and brown eyes like Chris, and he sported a beard Santa would have envied. He looked biker tough, but he really was a teddy bear.

"I've been good...and you guys?"

"Chris told us you interviewed him," Eileen said. "I have to admit, I'm hoping this might lead to a reunion." She winked at her.

"Sorry, Eileen, but I already have a boyfriend."

Her smile faded. "I hope he has the good sense to hang onto you, unlike my son over there." She pointed to Chris, who was standing by the kitchen door, talking to one of his waiters.

Isabel let out a nervous laugh. "It was good to see you both."

"You too, honey."

Mark gave her a Santa wave. "Take care."

When Isabel reached the exit, she turned toward Chris without thinking. He met her gaze, magnetically, and from the pout on his lips, he looked disappointed to see her go.

Her heart jumped with excitement.

That worried her beyond belief.

***

She arrived at the cemetery well past 8pm. A full moon and a blanket of stars lit the night sky. Clutch in hand, she followed the well-lit path to her dad's resting place.

"Hey, Dad." She placed a small bouquet of purple lilacs in the bronze vase next to her father's headstone. "I've been thinking about you a lot lately. There's so much I have to tell you and so many questions I wish you could answer."

She was about to mention the name Ethan when she felt a tap on her shoulder. She jumped a little before realizing it was Chris. "What are you doing here?"

"I'm on an extended break. Thought you might need this." He handed Isabel her cell phone. "You left it on the table."

"Oh my God..." She took the phone, careful not to touch his hand. "How stupid of me." She put it in her clutch.

"Where's your boyfriend, ah...Greg, right?"

"He's playing poker tonight."

"Oh. Sorry."

"It's okay. I usually come here alone, anyway."

"You come here a lot?"

"A couple times a month, and especially on the anniversary of his murder." She focused on the tombstone, shiny gray marble, white engraved letters: *Here lies Elliot Kingston.* "We have a lot to talk about."

"Like what?"

"I usually fill him in on what's going on in my life. But tonight, I'm mostly looking for answers."

"Answers?"

"I've been having these dreams where I'm with him when he dies. Each time, he whispers a name. I feel like he's trying to tell me something, maybe the name of his killer."

"In your dreams?"

"Yeah. In my dreams."

He frowned. "From the grave?"

"You don't believe me?"

"Hey." He put up his hands. "If you believe it, that's all that counts."

"Liv and her team reopened the case."

"That's a good idea."

"Greg doesn't agree. He's afraid that if Liv doesn't find the killer, I'll spiral into a depression."

Chris nodded. "I understand his concern, but I've known you for a long time, Bel. No matter what happens, I know you'll be fine."

"How could you know that?" she snapped. "You weren't there for me."

"I saw how you handled yourself after your dad died. You were stronger than I could ever be."

"No, Chris. I wasn't strong. You saw what I wanted you to see. The truth is, I cried myself to sleep every night."

"I'm sorry, Bel. I...I should have paid more attention."

"You shouldn't have left. You have no idea how badly you hurt me." Now she was shouting. "I needed you, Chris."

"I'm here now."

"Six years too late." She glared at him.

No, Isabel. Stop harping on him. He might think you care.

"You're right. I screwed up, and you moved on. My loss."

"Yeah, I have, and Greg will never walk out on me. So...so maybe you should just leave." She turned away from him.

Turn around, Isabel. Tell him the truth. You missed him every day but now it's too late.

"Before I go. I brought this for you."

She turned back around. Tears had flooded her eyes. He held out a container from his restaurant. "The cheesecake I told you about."

"I already had some."

"Have some more...or leave it for your dad."

She took the container but remained silent, though every part of her heart was screaming for him to gather her in his arms and tell her everything was going to be alright. He turned and walked away, and she let him go, even as she fought the urge to run to him and fall into his arms.

When he was out of sight, she turned to the stone cold effigy of her loving father. "Oh, Dad. What is wrong with me?" She fell on her knees and sobbed. "I should be happy that he's gone. Now Greg and I can move forward, be happy again."

That's all she wanted. Happiness with Greg. He could offer her adoration and dependability. What could Chris offer her besides broken hearts and dashed dreams and... "Cheesecake?"

It's damn good cheesecake, Dad.

She held the food container to her heart and cried.

What does it matter now? He's gone. The assignment is over. Greg's waiting for me at home. Put a period on it, girl, and move on.

Chapter 9

Isabel pulled her car into the driveway. Her dash clock read *9:15*. She was late but Greg's car wasn't anywhere to be seen. Worry rattled her nerves. He may have tired waiting for her and left.

She gathered her clutch and the cheesecake container, locked the car, and climbed the few steps to her dark porch. Before she could unlock the front door—

"You're late."

Fright kicked up her heartbeat and bristled the hairs on the back of her head. She damn near dropped the cheesecake. The voice had come from a deck chair at the end of the porch.

"Jesus, Greg. You scared the crap out of me. Where's your car?"

"I parked down the block to surprise you." He materialized from the darkness, walking toward her.

"Color me surprised." She set the

cheesecake and her clutch on the brick banister and, as her pounding heart settled, wrapped her arms around his neck. His cologne bedazzled her and smelled like home. "But am I ever glad to see you." On her tippy-toes, she found his lips in the darkness. His arms looped around her, and all was as it should be. No Chris, no murdered father, just passion in the arms of the man she loved. She pressed her cheek to his chest. "I missed you."

"Wow. I should play poker more often."

She giggled. It felt good to have her witty and loving boyfriend back. "How was your poker game?"

"I lost." Greg laughed.

"Want some cheesecake?" She pointed to the container on the banister.

"Is it from Chris's restaurant?"

"Yes."

"Then no thanks."

She shrugged. "More for me then." After unlocking the door, she picked up the cheesecake and clutch and led the way inside. As she walked to the kitchen to grab a fork, Greg made himself at home on the couch. It suddenly occurred to her that he didn't smell like he'd been playing poker with the guys. No beer on his breath, no cigar smoke on his shirt—

Her cell phone rang inside her clutch. She dug it out and saw it was Liv on the caller ID. "Hey, girlfriend, what's up?"

"I know you told me not to go all detective on Greg, but I did some digging."

"Seriously, Liv? You promised—"

"You can be mad at me later. Right now you need to listen. He's not who he says he is."

"What are you talking about?

"Trust me. His name isn't Greg Pearson. It's Ethan Bradley."

She felt the blood drain from her face. "Ethan?" she whispered.

The Ethan? That Ethan?

Her mouth turned to sand. "How do you know—"

"I'll explain later. Just don't piss him off before we get the warrant for his arrest."

"Arrest?" Isabel steadied her hand so her phone wouldn't shake and fought to remain calm. The earth had just dropped from beneath her feet. Her kitchen took on an awkward tilt. A glance to the living room told her he was still sitting on the couch. She couldn't let him know that she knew his real name.

"Isabel? You there?"

She had to think fast. "Ah...no worries. We can have lunch next week instead."

"Lunch?" She paused, then: "He's in the house, isn't he."

"Yeah, sounds good. No big deal."

"Listen to me, Bel. It's a big deal. He killed your father."

That was a punch in the gut. "No way. How—?" Her brain went on overload.

Not Greg. He's my boyfriend. I love him. In what cruel world could he be a killer?

"I'm ten minutes away and bringing backup. Don't hang up. Put your phone in your back pocket so I can hear what's going on."

"I can't—"

"Is everything okay?" Ethan asked from behind her.

Startled, she spun around. "Ah...yeah... Liv had to cancel our lunch plans for tomorrow." She slipped her 'hot' phone into her back pocket. "You sure you don't want some cheesecake?"

He scowled. "You know what I love about you?"

She forced a smile... "What's that?" and opened the cheesecake box. "Doesn't it smell delicious?"

"You're good at so many things." He leaned in close to her. "But the one thing you're not good at...is lying."

"Lying?" Her voice quivered. "Where did that come from?"

"You're white as a sheet and your hands are trembling. A canceled lunch date is never that shocking. I'll bet your detective friend ran a background check on me. Am I right?" He reached around her hip, pulled the phone from her pocket, and threw it on the floor. "What did she tell you?"

"Hey, if you broke my phone, you're paying for it."

Ethan leaned in so close she felt the heat of his breath on her face. "She told you something." His eyes were stern with fury. "I can tell...you're afraid of me."

"What the hell are you doing?"

"Isabel, I could never hurt you. I love you."

"Love me?" Anger gave her a shot of

courage. "Then tell me the truth. Is your real name Ethan?"

"I knew it." His lips tightened and his eyes narrowed. "She's trying to destroy everything we have together."

"Liv didn't kill my father. You did."

"Damn it." He shoved her back into the counter, pressed his body against hers, and slammed a fist on the counter top. "You weren't supposed to find out. I love you."

"You were stalking me all this time."

"I was not," he shouted. "I was dating you."

"All you wanted was a piece of ass from the daughter of the man you killed. What am I, your own private Mount Everest?"

"I know you're mad..." his voice softened, "you have every right to be, but don't you see? Our lives crossing paths this way was destiny. I knew it the moment you told me about your father. I couldn't believe it. What are the odds? It had to be divine intervention. We're meant to be together, don't you see?"

"You're delusional. I could never love you now."

"No. Don't say that. I love you. You love

me. Nothing's changed. We just have a little secret between us, is all."

"You're going to prison, Ethan."

"You're not listening to me," he screamed. "It's Chris, isn't it. He's turned you against me."

"Liv is on the way, and she's not coming alone."

"I didn't mean to kill him. I just wanted his money. Times were bad back then. I was desperate. But that's all behind me now. I've cleaned up. I've changed. It's a miracle how my life turned around. We can still be together, in love like we are, destined to get married and live happily ever after."

"Over my dead body." She pushed him away.

"That can be arranged." He pulled a knife from the butcher-block on the counter, grabbed the back of her neck and yanked her face to his. "If I can't have you, Chris isn't getting you, either." He planted his lips on her mouth and plunged the knife into her stomach.

She choked on the searing heat of the cold steel blade. Her brain got all jumbled up, unable to comprehend what he'd just done, but knowing it couldn't be taken back. Not now. Not ever. The kitchen lights dimmed, sounds became echoes... Even the thud her body made as it hit the floor didn't sound real. Surely it couldn't be *her* body...he loved her...but somehow that love had turned to hate and violence...

"Now look what you made me do," he yelled. "You should have forgiven me, let bygones be bygones, but no. You had to be all smarty pants, miss goody-two-shoes, better than me. It's all your fault."

Liv stormed in and scrambled toward her. Uniformed officers threw Ethan to the floor, piled on, and cuffed his hands behind his back.

"She did it," he yelled while writhing on the floor. "She stabbed herself. I tried to stop her. She's not well. She needs help."

Liv dropped to her knees and cradled Isabel's head in her arms. "Bel, stay with me."

Feeling weak and floating in a gray fog, she squeezed Liv's hand. *How bad is it?* That's when she realized she couldn't speak.

"Don't you dare die on me."

***

Isabel opened her eyes. She felt groggy and disoriented, and her entire body ached. Inhaling antiseptic air, she glanced around the dimly lit room, saw a counter and a sink, heard a beeping machine, and realized she was lying in a hospital bed.

What? How? When did I? That's when it came back in a quick flash. Greg with a knife in his hand, pulling her to him and shoving the knife into her stomach. She felt nauseous.

Liv and Chris were sitting in chairs on the other side of the room. Heads lolled against each other, they seemed to be asleep.

Her heart was pounding. She wasn't surprised to see Liv, but Chris? After everything she said at the cemetery, he still showed up. She wanted to get up, kiss his cheek, let him know how much it meant to have him there, but her body was so heavy and weak there was no way her feet could support her.

"How long have I been out?" she muttered.

They both popped out of their chairs. "Bel, oh my God." Liv rushed to her bedside. "How are you feeling?"

"My boyfriend stabbed me. I've been better."

"I was so worried. I thought I'd lost you."

"It was touch and go for a while," Chris said, walking around to the other side of the bed. He took her hand and gently stroked her fingers. A few days ago, his touch would have caused her to flinch and pull away, maybe lash out. Today she found herself in need of his tenderness and didn't want him to stop. She kept her hand still, but averted her eyes.

"We got him," Liv said.

"You did it. You solved my dad's murder."

Liv's eyes teared up. "I had a strange feeling when I first met him at dinner, especially when he claimed to be on the wrestling team at North Eastern. I attended every match...didn't see anyone who looked like him. So, when you two were smooching, I took his salad fork to be tested for DNA. While I waited on the lab results, I called

NE's athletic department. They had no record of Greg Pearson ever attending that school."

"Was he ever in Boston?"

"He grew up in Philly...worked at an advertising agency, as a janitor, got fired for verbally attacking a supervisor, the day before your dad was murdered."

Isabel looked at the I-V needle in the back of her hand, felt grateful she'd fared better than her father did, after a knife attack. "How did you solve the case?"

"His DNA matched the DNA found on your dad's wallet. We didn't have a name to go with the DNA, until now. When I ran a background check on Greg Pearson, I found a cross reference to a domestic violence case from ten years ago. I pulled up the case file. A Becky Smith was assaulted by her boyfriend, Ethan Bradley, and he had a rap-sheet a mile long."

Chris said, "No wonder he changed his name."

"I contacted Becky Smith. She lives in Montana now. My god, she fell apart at the mention of Ethan's name. She told me he often made her call him Greg Pearson and pretend he'd just picked her up at a bar for some 'stranger sex.' He liked to rough her up. She'd finally had enough and reported his abuse. He served two years in prison. That was before DNA was taken from felons and logged into a national database. He worked at the advertising agency for almost a year before he got fired."

"He said it was destiny that we met, and we were meant to be together."

"Destiny?" Chris asked.

"He's a narcissistic ass," Liv put in.

"My father warned me about Ethan, in my dreams. I thought they were nightmares until I realized they were messages from my dad."

Chris squeezed her hand. "Sorry I didn't believe you."

Liv patted Isabel's arm. "Don't you worry. Ethan's going away for a long time."

Isabel let out a deep sigh. "So, was anything he'd said about himself true?"

"None of it, but the odd thing is, he actually earned a degree in journalism from UPenn. He'd turned his life completely around since the murder."

Isabel huffed. "I was such a fool."

"Don't blame yourself," Chris said. "I never liked the guy, but I didn't see this coming."

"It's over," Liv put in. "Now you need to concentrate on getting well."

Chris leaned in close. "I know I screwed up, and I'm sorry, but I'm here for you now. Anything you need."

"I'll need a lot of attention. You've got a restaurant to run, a successful business that needs you. How do I know you won't leave me again?"

Chris looked like he was about to say something when a doctor walked in. "Sorry to interrupt. I just need to check on our patient." He strode to the bed. "I'm Doctor Wolfe. How are you feeling, Ms. Kingston?"

"Happy to be alive."

"Surgery went well, got the bleeding stopped and patched up your colon, could have been worse, but it'll be a while before you're fully recovered."

"When can I go home?"

"First things first. We'll monitor your condition and take it from there."

"Thanks for saving my life."

"My pleasure." He'd said it as if his

miracles were an everyday occurrence. "I'll check on you later."

"I should go too." Liv leaned down to give Isabel a gentle kiss on her forehead. "I'm really glad you're going to be okay."

"Thanks to you."

"I'll follow you out," Chris said.

Once she was alone with the beeping heart monitor and the lingering pain in her stomach, she closed her eyes and hoped to dream of her father so she could thank him too.

Chapter 10

Isabel had been awake for an hour, staring out the window from her hospital bed. She focused on the beautiful morning and the white fluffy clouds floating in the sky. One cloud resembled the pet fish she had when she was five. It was better to focus on Miss Mildred than the pain from her stab wound.

Nurse Cassie walked in with a cheerful smile. For someone who worked in a hospital, she had an impressive amount of energy. She bounced to Isabel's bedside, her ponytail swaying from side to side. "How's your pain level on a scale from one to five, five being the worst."

Isabel winced and held up five fingers.

"Hold on, hon, I'll get you something for it." She gathered up Isabel's food tray, Jell-O cup, and napkins then left the room.

Five days ago I almost died.

Nurse Cassie returned with a little paper

cup with two pills in it. "Down the hatch." She handed Isabel a sippy cup.

"You're an angel." Isabel swallowed the pills.

"I bet you're excited to be leaving today."

"I miss my own bed."

Cassie laughed. "I'm going to miss you, Isabel, but I'm glad you're going to be okay."

"The feeling is mutual."

"I'll be back shortly to help you get discharged."

Isabel tilted her head to the side to stare out the window again. She smiled as she pictured herself lying in her comfy queen size bed, hugging her extra pillow. Then she shuddered when Ethan's face popped into her daydream. Her heart began to race and her palms became sweaty. She'd made love to Ethan in that bed. Now she wanted to burn the sheets.

His preliminary hearing was in a couple of days. Against her better judgment, she planned to attend. She dreaded the idea of being in the same room as that monster, but she needed to see justice play out and wanted to be present when a trial date was set.

Maybe he'd plead guilty and be done with it. Fingers crossed.

"Up and at 'em," Nurse Cassie said.

Isabel hadn't seen her come in, but the familiar voice brought her back to the present. Her heart rate slewed back to its normal pace.

"I have your discharge instructions ready. Shall we get started?"

"Absolutely."

They were all a bit overwhelming, information regarding diet, "Eat plenty of protein," pain meds, "no driving, no alcohol," and incision care, "Don't lift anything over ten pounds. Call the hospital if you have any questions." She handed Isabel the list of instructions, along with a prescription for pain medication and another for an antibiotic. "Do you have someone coming to pick you up?"

"That would be me." Chris was standing in the doorway, holding the handles of a wheelchair.

"I thought Liv was coming to get me."

"Change of plans." He wheeled the chair

to her bedside.

She frowned. "Liv should have warned me."

"Look, Bel, you were right. Six years ago, I was selfish and stupid..."

"Go on. Give me a good excuse for breaking my heart."

"I'm here now, and I promise I won't leave you again."

"Why should I trust your word? We had plans—"

"We did, but right now, you got stabbed and you need someone to take care of you. May as well be me."

Nurse Cassie said, "He makes a good point."

"Cassie, did you miss the part about how he broke my heart?"

"Hey. At least he didn't stab you in the stomach."

Isabel didn't know what hurt worse, but they were ganging up on her because they cared. "Okay, Chris, but no funny business." She pointed a stern finger at him.

"Fair enough." He levered up the wheelchair's foot pads. "Now let's get you home."

***

An hour later, Chris pulled his SUV into Isabel's driveway and parked next to her car. "Are you ready to go inside?"

She inhaled. "I can make it."

He walked around to the passenger side door, opened it, and carefully helped Isabel out. He wrapped a strong left arm around her waist while she hooked her right arm around his neck.

As he slowly walked her to the front porch, she glanced up at him, happy to have him with her, though she wasn't ready to admit it to him, yet. He stopped at the steps. "Here comes the hard part."

"I got it."

One step at a time, she made the porch. The front door was unlocked, which struck her as being odd. Did they not lock up after the assault?

Inside, Liv was waiting for them. A *WELCOME HOME* banner hung on the dining room wall, and a vase of flowers sat on the table. Though all traces of the knife attack had been cleaned up, the sense of insecurity in her own home still lingered.

She wanted to turn around and run outside, run down the street screaming...but she refused to let Ethan have that much control over her emotions.

Liv rushed to her and wrapped her in a tender hug. "Welcome home."

"Thanks, Liv. But how did you get in?"

"I used the spare key you keep under the mat. By the way, you shouldn't do that. Burglars know where to look for keys."

"Yes, detective."

Chris helped her into a dining room chair. "I'll let you ladies handle it from here." He handed Liv the discharge instructions and the pharmacy bag of prescriptions.

"Thanks for picking her up."

"My pleasure." He turned to Isabel. "My shift starts tomorrow morning. I'll see you then."

"I'm holding you to that."

He chuckled then waved goodbye.

After he left, Isabel looked around the room. To think she might not have ever seen her place again reminded her of her mortality. Life was short and never guaranteed. She took a deep breath and noticed the underlying scent of bleach mingling with her tropical breeze air freshener.

"Are you hungry?" Liv asked

"For anything but hospital food."

Liv placed the pharmacy bag on the table, next to a crystal vase of pink roses. A small card nestled within the blossoms: *Get Well Soon— Chris.*

Her mouth opened slightly as she placed her hand over her heart. "How sweet of him." She heard the fridge door shut.

"I think he's in it to win it." Liv walked to the table, carrying three large restaurant carry-out containers, each one labeled with a different entree.

Isabel's eyes widened. Chris was pulling out all the stops.

"Take your pick." Liv opened the lids.

"That one." *Trout and risotto.*

"Coming right up." She took it to the kitchen and fired up the microwave.

"Chris brought all this food over?"

"There's more." Liv pointed to the fridge.

"He really wants me to forgive him."

Liv smiled. "All in the name of love."

"What? No."

"Oh, come on, Bel. That guy is still crazy about you, and don't tell me you don't feel the same way about him."

"Of course not." Isabel felt her cheeks heat. "He broke my heart."

"Boo-hoo. That was a long time ago, Bel. You both have grown a lot since then. You owe it to yourself to give him a chance."

Isabel grimaced as her stomach reacted to her advice. "I'm done with men for a while. Don't trust any of them."

"Can't say I blame you." Liv returned from the kitchen with two steaming entrées and set a plate in front of Isabel. "How about I give you a foot massage." She sat catty-corner from her. "You can lie back, close your eyes, talk or don't talk. Your choice."

"That sounds nice."

After lunch, Liv cleared the table then helped Isabel to the couch. She grabbed two pillows, one to place behind her neck and another for under her feet.

As Liv began the massage, Isabel tilted her head back and closed her eyes. She felt a tingling sensation as the tension in her muscles subsided and peace settled into her mind. She'd worry about Ethan and Chris some other time, but for now, life was all about Liv and her busy fingers.

After the massage, Liv grabbed the TV remote off the coffee table and searched the channels until she found a rom-com to watch: *Sleepless in Seattle*.

As the closing credits rolled, Isabel yawned. "I don't know about you, but I'm wiped."

"Gee, I don't know why," Liv joked. She helped Isabel up, walked her to the bedroom, and helped her into her p-jays. "You'll have to go to the bathroom by yourself. I don't get paid enough to help you with that."

With Isabel tucked in and resting comfortably in her bed, Liv walked back out to the living room to get the overnight bag she had placed near the TV stand. After getting dressed for bed, she climbed in next to Isabel and cozied up under the blanket, like it was just another high-school sleepover.

"So," Isabel said. "What's the update on Jack?"

"I thought you were tired."

"Curious, is all. Has he asked you out?"

"Actually, I asked *him* out."

"Good for you. Where are you going?"

"Dinner and a concert. Jack got us tickets to see our favorite band this weekend, in New York."

"That sounds expensive."

"I'll make it worth every dime."

Isabel giggled. Hearing Liv talk about her blossoming relationship with Jack made her think of Chris and their train wreck of a romance. He'd be here tomorrow. She'd be alone with him. An intimate setting with no distractions and plenty of time to talk.

Maybe Liv was right. Maybe he did deserve another chance, but what would that cost her in the end? Couldn't be worse than the price she'd paid for loving Greg.

Chapter 11

The next morning, Isabel awoke with a rumbling stomach. Liv's sleeping spot was empty, the sheets and comforter pulled up as if she were never there. Isabel's impulse was to rise from her bed, as she would on any given day, but the moment she pushed herself up, pain drove her back down.

I can do this.

A second attempt failed, and her head fell back on the pillow.

I can't do this.

She glanced to the nightstand to check the time. *8:05am*. Next to the clock sat a glass of water and two pills Liv had set out for her. She reached for them and managed to hold her head up enough to swallow the meds. It could be as long as twenty minutes for relief to kick in. Lying there, she had to wonder if she'd be in good enough shape to make Ethan's preliminary hearing, set for tomorrow morning. No matter what, missing it was not an option. If it was going to hurt then, she may as well get used to the pain now. That was enough motivation to force herself to sit up.

She heard clinking down the hall, what sounded like plates and silverware being placed on the table. "Liv? Chris?"

Chris rushed in wearing a flour-dusted apron. "Good. You're awake. How do you feel?"

"Something smells delicious."

"Pancakes, hash browns, and sliced strawberries. Are you hungry?"

She held out her hand. "Help me to the bathroom first."

He walked her to the door. She was surprised at how well she managed to walk, a bit stooped but ambulatory enough to get around on her own. He left her to take care of business, after which she shuffled herself to the dining room.

Chris pulled a chair out for her, and she sat down to a banquet laid out in front of her.

"Do you remember the first time I made this breakfast for you?" he whispered seductively, his breath tickling her ear.

"Our second week of college. You stayed the weekend, while my roommate was away."

"My favorite part was what happened *after* breakfast." He winked.

"We were solid, until you left and ruined everything."

"I like to think we were only temporarily on hold."

"Think what you like. I've got bigger things to worry about than your groveling."

"What could be more important than me with egg on my face?"

"I'm anxious about Ethan's preliminary hearing tomorrow. What if he makes bail?"

Chris sighed. "You won't be alone. Your mom, Bill, Liv, and I will all be there with you."

"That helps to know."

"In the meantime, I thought it might be good to get out of the house for a bit."

"What did you have in mind?"

"A picnic at the park. Do you think you can manage to walk a little ways?"

"It'll be good practice for court tomorrow. Let's eat breakfast first."

***

That afternoon, she and Chris slowly walked arm-in-arm into Clark Park. He carried a picnic cooler in his free hand. A gentle breeze rustled her purple sundress. Thankfully, her stomach pains weren't severe enough to forego this excursion.

Children were running across the grass, playing a game of tag, while their parents sat close by. One young man threw a Frisbee for his black Lab. The dog jumped in the air and made an incredible catch. Two elderly men sat at a table nearby, enjoying a quiet game of chess.

Isabel tilted her head up to Chris. He was wearing a white polo shirt and tan shorts. The scent of his Nautica cologne teased her senses. "This was a good idea."

He grinned. "I'm full of them."

"Oh yeah? What was your last good idea?"

"To buy a boat."

"You have a boat?"

"A pontoon boat. The *MackenSEA*. And she's a beauty."

"I don't recall you having an interest in

boats."

"I went out once, in Ohio, on the river with a cook, and found it to be a good escape from the stress of my job."

"I thought you loved working in your restaurants."

"I do, but the responsibilities can take a toll on my nerves. Too much salt here, not enough salt there, what's taking so long? Wait staff wants more money and chefs want more creative liberty. Mop the floor, clean the counter. My boat is where I go to recharge."

"Will you take me sometime?" The words were out before she realized her mistake. A date with Chris was not in her future plans.

He looked at her sideways. "Ah...sure, since you're interested. I keep her at the Pier 3 Marina."

"Maybe when I get better."

"Are you getting hungry?"

"I could eat."

An empty table stood a few feet away. He removed a couple pb&j sandwiches from the picnic cooler, a big bag of chips, and two bottles of water. "I decided to forgo packing the champagne on account of your meds."

"Good call." She took a bite of her sandwich. "I haven't been to this park in years. Never had the time, until now. I...almost died." Her eyes glistened with tears.

Chris slowly reached out his hand to wipe away a tear. "You're going to be fine."

She smiled as a way of letting him know it was okay to touch her. Closing her eyes, she used her hand to keep his in place. The intimacy of his touch felt good. It felt right. Even the sun agreed as it captured the moment in its warm rays.

She took a few more bites of her sandwich and a couple sips of her water then pushed the half-eaten meal away.

Chris started shuffling around, packing up the remnants of their lunch while she simply relaxed.

"We should head back now." He extended his hand to help her up.

"Do we have to go?"

"You've had enough sun for one day."

"Yeah." She sighed. "Back to four walls."

"You don't want to go home?"

"It's too beautiful a day to waste it lying

in bed."

"How would you like a tour of my new place?"

She'd already suffered enough sexual tension between them. A house tour could be dangerous territory, but considering her current predicament, she decided to throw caution to the wind. "I'd love that."

"Great." Chris helped her up, but she managed to walk on her own power the short distance back to the car. He opened the passenger door and let her hold his hand for support as she got seated inside.

Isabel stared out the window as he drove. During the six years that they'd been apart, Chris had developed a whole new side to himself, a side she wished she could have been a part of as it developed.

She took a long, deep breath. One thing was for sure. It was his choice to leave her behind when he flew off to make his fortune. He didn't only break her heart, he stole six years of shared experiences. They should have grown and changed together. Instead, if they would ever be a couple again, she'd have to jump aboard the moving train that his life had become.

Chapter 12

Chris pulled into his driveway, and Isabel's eyes widened. His house was a white colonial with blue shutters and a wrap-around front porch that overlooked a manicured front yard adorned with colorful flowerbeds and sprawling oaks. It was easy to picture him sitting on the veranda in one of the tan cushioned armchairs, sipping his morning coffee and reading the news on his laptop.

Chris helped her out of the car and kept a ready hand at her waist in case she had trouble walking straight. She was hunched over a bit more than at the park and bumped into him a few times as they were walking to the front door.

"Are you in pain?"

"Some but not too bad."

"Maybe this is too much for one day. I should take you home."

"I'm okay. Let's keep moving."

Inside, her eyes were immediately drawn to the living room. In the center, he'd set a gray sectional with a chaise extension and three blue accent pillows. A round glass coffee table sat in front of it. Across from the ensemble, a flat-screen TV hung on an eggshell-white wall above a stone and mortar fireplace.

"I feel like I need to take my shoes off."

Chris laughed. "That's not necessary." He motioned for her to follow him and stopped at the arched doorway to the kitchen. "This is my favorite room in the house."

"I can see why."

It was the perfect kitchen for anyone in the restaurant business: pristine marble counter tops, wall shelves holding dozens of cookbooks, and all new polished chrome appliances.

She toured three bedrooms, two-and-a-half baths, and a basement that could easily be turned into a separate apartment.

Once the tour was complete, Chris led her back to the living room. "What do you think?"

"It's beautiful but..."

"But what?"

"Can we sit down?"

"Sure." He motioned to the couch.

She got comfortable, took a breath, then: "This house, your boat, and everything you've acquired in the last six years is amazing, but it's yours. It's your life, but it could have been ours, house shopping together, deciding on the paint for the walls, the tile in the bathrooms, the name for your boat. I'm just a guest in your world, and that's all I'll ever be."

"I've always regretted how I let things end between us, and I wish I could go back to that moment and ask you to come with me."

She placed her hand on his. "You know I would have said yes. Why didn't you?"

"Because I knew you would have said yes."

"It's not a Catch-22 question, Chris."

"Your whole life is here in Philly, and sure, maybe you would have been happy in Ohio, at first anyway, but eventually you would have started to miss everything and everyone you left behind. It would have been selfish of me to ask you to come along."

"You had no right to make that decision for me. You left me with nothing but heartache, but to be honest, since you've been back, I've been fighting one simple fact. I've never stopped loving you."

"Fighting it? Why?"

"I'm not the same woman you walked away from. I stand up for myself now, protect my heart, and I won't let you shatter it again."

"I can't blame you for that."

She sat there staring at him, just inches apart. Her eyes lighted on his heavenly lips.

He met her stare, then brought his hands to her cheeks and leaned in.

"Don't."

Do. Please, do.

He started to lean away.

She grabbed the back of his head and pulled his lips to hers. They tasted like home, a place as far away as the moon now plummeting back to earth in a fiery wave of heat and want. She knew she was playing with fire, dropping her guard and letting herself get burned. His probing tongue was the devil's finger coaxing her to jump in, tempting her to abandon all caution to the hot winds of passion. There'd be no escape, no turning back. Her fast-beating heart was warning her of the danger, but her mouth wasn't listening, just diving in for more and more of the love she'd lost so long ago. The same could not be said for her stomach, as the butterflies flitting about had wings of sharp glass, cutting and slicing at the core of her wounds. She pushed back from heaven's door and inhaled a painful breath. "We have to stop before I blow out my stitches."

His face flushed. "You're right." He scooted back. "What was I thinking?"

"That you're still in love with me."

"Good guess. To be continued then?"

"Please take me home."

"Yes, ma'am."

***

By the time Chris drove Isabel back to her house, it was past 6pm. She was hungry. Her pb&j sandwich for lunch had worn off hours ago.

After she settled into a chair at the table, Chris walked to the kitchen and pulled open the refrigerator door. "How does buttered noodles and tuna sound?"

"Perfect."

As the microwave whirred, she checked her phone for messages, thinking Liv might have news on tomorrow's preliminary hearing. No news was good news.

Chris returned with two steaming plates. "I'll get you some ice water." He was gone again, as if he was a waiter and she was his restaurant patron.

After dinner, Chris cleared the table while she retreated to the couch in the living room. His tinkering in the kitchen got her to thinking about their history and how so little of it survived the breakup. She'd kept it in a box for safekeeping.

"Can I get you anything?" he asked when he joined her.

"There's something I want to show you." She got up off the couch. "I'll be right back."

He sat down and picked up the TV remote, but before he could choose a show, she returned from the bedroom with a pink shoe box. He tweaked his brows curiously.

"After we broke up, I threw out most of

the stuff that reminded me of you." She set the box on the coffee table and knelt beside it. "But I couldn't bring myself to get rid of it all."

He sat forward and braced his forearms on his knees. "What have you got there?"

She pulled four items from the box and set them on the table: a dried rose from their first Valentine's Day together, the carnival ticket from their first date, a picture of the happy youngsters at their senior prom, and the blue heart-necklace he'd given her for her 18th birthday.

He picked up the prom picture, studied it then smiled. "That was a great night."

"The limo, the live band, and no morning hangovers."

"I think we were two of the few sober seniors there."

She took the picture back from him, and seeing their youthfulness and the hopes and dreams in their eyes, she returned it to the box where everything lost belonged. Next, she picked up the necklace and ran her thumb over the heart. How ironic that it was as blue as their romance had ended.

"You used to wear that all the time."

"Sometimes I slept with it on. It killed me to pack these memories away."

He took the necklace from her and clasped it around her neck. "This doesn't go back in the box." He joined her on the floor.

Her eyes got all teary. She picked up the Valentine's rose, its pedals as dry and dead as their love had become. And the carnival ticket, worthless but priceless at the same time. "Why did you do this to us?" she sobbed out.

"Bel, come on. You're torturing yourself with this stuff." He put the rose and the ticket in the box with the old photo and shut the lid. "Let's look to the future and not the past."

She wrapped her arms around his neck and cried into his ear. "I don't know how I can forget what you did to us."

"I think you need some sleep." He lifted her from the floor and led her down the hall to the bathroom to change her bandage. Everything he needed was laid out on the counter. He unzipped her dress and let it fall around her ankles, leaving her in bra and panties with a white bandage between them.

She felt a bit embarrassed, needing him

in this way, but her body wasn't anything he hadn't seen before.

He cut the bandage in back, looped it around to the front, and peeled the gauze pad from the wound. Ethan Bradley's mark on her would never entirely go away. "Let me know if I'm hurting you."

He was so caring and tender with her as he applied the antibacterial salve and set a new gauze pad over it. "You doing alright?"

"I think you chose the wrong profession. Your sink-side manner is impeccable."

"Maybe in another life." He wrapped her torso with a new length of white bandage and secured it with medical tape. "How's that feel? Not too tight?"

She looked at herself in the mirror, the mess Ethan had made of her body, and broke out in a fresh wave of tears. How had she been so foolish?

Please, God. Make this nightmare end.

Chapter 13

The next morning, Isabel's hands were shaking as she sat in Chris's parked SUV outside the courthouse. She had to steel every nerve in her body to face her attacker again.

Meredith and Bill were sitting in the back seat.

Chris placed his hand on top of hers. "Everything's going to be okay. He can't hurt you."

She took a deep shaky breath. "I know. You're right."

"It's not too late to leave," her mother said. "You're not required to attend a preliminary hearing."

She shook her head. "I need to be here...to show that bastard that I'm going to watch him go down for what he did to me."

Chris stepped out and opened the door for Isabel. She got out and clung to his arm, but not just for physical support. His closeness kept her from falling apart.

Liv was waiting for them outside the courthouse doors. She was wearing a gray pantsuit with her hair pulled back. Her arms were open for Isabel, who felt like she was bleeding through her white short-sleeved dress. "I'm proud of you, Bel. This takes courage."

Isabel touched her blue heart necklace and stroked it with her fingertips. "Okay, let's do this."

Entering the courtroom, Isabel felt nauseous. Every footstep was an echo within the wood-paneled walls. People were seated in church-like pews. Ethan, dressed in a red jumpsuit, sat at a table on the right of the judge's bench.

Liv had roped off a row up front for her and the family. She sat next to Chris and clasped his hand.

Ethan turned to look at her, smiled, and mouthed *I love you.*

She wanted to punch that smirk off his face.

Please let this go well.

The judge struck the gavel plate. "The

court will come to order. We're here today for a preliminary hearing in the case of the state of Pennsylvania versus Ethan Bradley. The defendant is charged with assault with a deadly weapon and attempted second degree murder. May I remind everyone, this is not a trial. I'm tasked with determining whether or not there's enough evidence to take the case to trial. The defended is presumed innocent. Is the state ready to proceed?"

The prosecutor stood, a tall slim woman in suit and tie. "Yes, your Honor. We have evidence the defendant, Ethan Bradley used a kitchen knife to stab Isabel Kingston in the stomach." She held up an evidence bag containing the bloody knife. "The ME has confirmed that the blood on the weapon is Ms. Kingston's blood, and Mr. Bradley's finger and palm prints are on the handle. We are also prepared to present testimony from the detective who arrived on scene mere seconds after the stabbing. We're also prepared to present doctors who will testify to the severity of the wounds inflicted by the knife we have in evidence." She sat down.

The judge turned his attention to Ethan's counselor. "And what say you for the defense?"

A fat guy with a bald crown stood next to Ethan. "Your Honor, the prosecution is contending that my client, Ethan Bradley, attacked Ms. Kingston. This couldn't be farther from the truth. We concede that she was injured, but my client was nothing short of loving and attentive to Ms. Kingston. Mr. Bradley and Ms. Kingston were in a relationship. We're prepared to show evidence that Ms. Kingston was mentally unstable at the time, distraught over her father's murder, and that she attempted suicide with that kitchen knife."

"Objection." The prosecutor stood. "We've seen no such evidence of mental deficiency, your Honor. The defense is grandstanding."

"Overruled. We'll sort this out later. Continue, counselor."

Isabel squeezed Chris's hand. "I'm not crazy. Ethan's trying to make this out to be all my fault."

"Relax. He's desperate."

The counselor added, "We have proof

the prosecution's witness, Detective Olivia Morris, fabricated evidence implicating my client in a cold case murder."

"Objection."

"Sustained," the judge shouted. "A cold case murder is irrelevant in this case."

Liv leaned to Isabel. "We're still preparing the case against Ethan for your father's murder. We'll get him locked up on this charge and arraign him on the murder charge later."

The defense counselor pushed back. "It calls to the victim's state of mind, your Honor. I would like to summon Dr. Theresa Gallo to the stand."

This isn't good.

Liv's leg began to bounce.

Dr. Gallo was sworn in and took the stand.

The defense counselor approached. "Dr. Gallo, you have been a highly respected psychiatrist in Philadelphia for twenty-five years. What area do you specialize in?"

"Grief counseling."

"Is it your professional opinion that someone with unresolved grief could have a mental break with reality, resulting in harm to themselves?"

"Every person handles grief differently. I would need to know the specifics before stating a professional opinion."

"A simple *yes* or *no* would suffice. Can a grieving person have a mental break?"

"Yes."

"Objection, your Honor. The victim isn't on trial here."

The counselor interjected. "I move to have all charges dropped, your Honor. The state has no case against my client. He should be released from custody immediately."

Isabel felt like she would vomit. "I need to get out of here." She stood and pulled Chris to his feet. He led her through the doors and into the hallway to a bench seat against the wall.

Isabel sniffled and wiped tears from her cheeks. "That attorney is making me sound like a deranged lunatic." She was shaking with anger.

"Everybody who matters knows the truth, and any jury worth their salt will see through the defense's lies."

"If the case goes to trial. He could walk

today. I wish Liv was ready to nail him for my dad's murder."

Liv, Meredith, and Bill walked out of the courtroom. They weren't smiling but they weren't frowning.

"So?" Isabel asked. "Is he going free?"

"It's not a slam-dunk case, but the good news is the judge ruled there's enough probable cause that a crime was committed and that Ethan committed that crime. He's bound over for trial."

Isabel exhaled. "Wow. I expected to be arrested for stabbing myself."

Liv set a hand on Isabel's shoulder. "The judge denied Ethan bail and remanded him to the Sheriff's department to await trial. Meanwhile, we'll set an arraignment date on the murder charge. He's not going anywhere."

Isabel felt relieved. "I need to see my dad."

Chris stood. "Sounds like we're going to the cemetery. How about lunch afterwards? My restaurant. My treat."

Outside the courthouse, Liv turned to Isabel. "I wish I could go with you guys, but I need to get back to work."

Isabel gave her a hug. "Thanks for solving my dad's murder."

"You're welcome." She headed for her squad car parked at the curb marked, *Police Vehicles Only.*

Isabel held Chris's arm as they walked back to his car, along with Meredith and Bill. After she got into the passenger seat, he gave her a kiss on the cheek. "I'm proud of you."

"For what?"

"Not puking in the courtroom. I swear your face was turning green."

"You know me so well."

Meredith and Bill climbed into the back seat. "Let's go," Bill said. "I'm hungry."

At the cemetery, Chris and Bill stayed in the car to give Isabel and her mom some alone-time with Elliot. Once she reached his grave, Isabel knelt down and smiled. "We did it, Dad. We caught your killer. He's going to stand trial."

Meredith stepped up and placed her hand on Elliot's tombstone. "You would have been so proud of our girl today. She sat there, in the courtroom, composed the whole time, even with that psychopath sitting so close to her."

"You have no idea how much we miss you, Dad." Isabel kissed the palm of her hand and placed it on her father's tombstone. "I'll see you in my dreams."

Meredith wiped away a tear. "I'll be back soon, dear."

As they walked back to the car, Isabel placed her head against her mother's shoulder. Her heart felt warm as she imagined her father walking next to them.

I will never be someone's victim again.

In that moment, she had an epiphany. She'd survived an attack once, but Ethan wasn't the only monster out there. She needed to protect herself.

She needed a gun.

Chapter 14

The next day, Isabel met Liv for lunch at *Penny's* Good Luck *Charm.* She'd given this a lot of thought, and decided it was time to approach Liv about getting a gun.

"What do you want a gun for?" Liv asked.

"After everything that's happened, I need a little extra protection."

"I don't disagree. I'm just surprised. Are you sure about this? Gun ownership is a huge responsibility."

"Ethan's the last time I let down my guard." She couldn't blame Liv for being skeptical. Isabel had always been against owning a gun of any kind. Now she worried about coming face-to-face with another psychopath and being defenseless.

Liv reached across the table and took hold of Isabel's hand. "I'll help you through the process. I know a great gun range where you can practice, and I can recommend a self defense class, if you'd like."

"That'd be great."

"Okay, enough of this heavy talk." Liv let go of her hand, to take a bite of her tuna melt. "How's everything going with Chris?"

"I told him how I felt, and he didn't take it badly."

Liv giggled like a school girl. "Are you just going to leave me hanging? What did he say?"

"He kissed me."

"Finally," she said, probably louder than she intended. "I assume that means you're back together?"

"We're playing it by ear." She took a bite of her grilled cheese sandwich. "He's invited me to dinner at his parents' house tonight. His mom is cooking."

"A home cooked meal from Mrs. Mackenzie? I'm jealous."

"Should be a fun night."

As much as she loved Chris's parents, she was a little nervous about having dinner with them. Logically, she knew there was no reason to be worried. They liked her as much as she liked them, but right now, the cautious part of her was in control.

***

Back at Isabel's house, she walked straight to her bedroom and opened the closet door. She had a few hours before Chris came to pick her up for dinner, but Liv couldn't stay long, and Isabel had difficulty getting dressed by herself.

She skimmed through her clothes a few times, until she found the outfit she wanted, a purple tee and soft black leggings. To complete the casual but athletic look, she selected the sterling-silver star-necklace her father had given her for her 21st birthday.

"You look great," Liv said.

They walked out of her room and took a seat on the couch.

"I was going to bring this up earlier but the conversation got away from me," Liv said. "The prosecution has offered Ethan a plea deal: fifteen years for assault with a deadly weapon, and they'd drop the attempted second degree murder charge. The defense has agreed. All the judge needs is the victim's approval. That would be you."

"Fifteen years for damn near killing me? Look what he did to me." Isabel pointed to her stomach. "That's not enough."

"It'll save you from testifying at trial and recounting the assault for a jury."

"And if I don't agree?"

"It'll go to trial, but like I said, it's no slam-dunk. He could get fifteen years or get off scot-free. Juries are unpredictable. They may buy the defense's attempted suicide argument, as I nor my team actually saw him stab you. This way, while he's sitting in a prison cell, we can hit him with the murder charge."

"It's a good plan, but I want to talk to my mom first. Can I get back to you?"

"Of course. I understand."

After Liv left, Isabel called her mom.

"What do you think?" she asked after she explained the plea deal to her mother.

"Honey, what Ethan did to our family was dreadful, but I wouldn't want to get up on that stand. The defense attorney will make the jury think it was your fault."

She took a deep breath and exhaled slowly. "Yeah. I need to put this behind me and move on with my life. Thanks, Mom."

"Any time, honey."

She hung up and called Liv."

"We agree to the plea deal, but you've got to charge him for my dad's murder."

"I think that's a smart move. I'll tell the DA and let you know the court date for Ethan's sentencing."

"Thanks."

Chris arrived to pick her up for dinner. "Don't be surprised if my mom is overly enthusiastic tonight. She's been gushing about us ever since I told her we were back together."

She laughed. "You sound pretty confident about that."

"I shouldn't be?"

"Chris, you know I care about you, but I can't trust you. I want to forgive you and get back to where we once were, but..."

"You're just not there yet. I get it."

"Let's just take our time. There's no rush, no pressure, no labels, boyfriend or girlfriend, just two people trying to get on with our lives."

"I understand, but my mom is really excited."

"In that case, I won't burst her bubble."

"Shall we go?"

***

The Mackenzie house was just as Isabel remembered it: a gray vinyl-sided ranch, paneled windows in the front, and a tall cherry tree standing in the center of a plush green lawn.

Mark came to the door just as Chris led her to the porch. "Hey, guys, great timing. Dinner is just about ready."

In the dining room, Chris pulled a chair out for her and she accepted it with a smile. He commandeered the chair next to her. The table was already set with Eileen's blue-patterned china, polished silverware, water glasses, and a bread basket.

"Isabel..." Eileen rushed from the kitchen to greet her with a hug and kiss on the cheek. "How are you doing, sweetheart?"

"I have my good days and bad, as far as the pain goes, but the doc says I'm healing up fine. It helps to know that Ethan can't hurt me or anyone else again."

Chris huffed. "You don't know that for sure."

"There's been a plea deal. He'll plead guilty, no trial. He'll go away for fifteen years, but after Liv pops the murder charge on him, he'll never see daylight again."

"I can't imagine the relief you must feel." Eileen walked back to the kitchen to retrieve the lasagna.

"I'm definitely relieved. I also have a lot of free time before I go back to work."

"When is that?" Mark asked.

"In six weeks. I should be good as new by then."

"What are you planning to do with all that spare time?" Eileen doled out the lasagna. It smelled divine. She sent a sly smile to Chris. "I imagine you'll be spending a lot of time with the people you love."

"Mom." Chris groaned.

"What? I can't be happy that you're back together?"

Isabel had to clench her jaw to refrain from blurting out the truth and busting Eileen's bubble. "Yes, I've been making a lot of plans with my mom and Liv, and of course this guy over here." She wrapped an arm around Chris's shoulders."

"With all you've been through, it might

be nice to go on a weekend getaway."

"Eileen," Mark said. "Let the poor girl eat." He heaped lasagna on his fork and levered it into his mouth.

Once they finished eating, Eileen led everyone to the living room where she regaled Isabel with a story from Chris's childhood.

"One year I volunteered to make a birthday cake for Chris's cousin Allie. Chris was six years old and liked to help in the kitchen, so of course, he wanted to help bake the cake."

"Of course." Isabel grinned at Chris.

Mark rolled his eyes. "Eileen, I've heard this story a hundred times."

Eileen gave him a stern look. "And you'll hear it again." She turned back to Isabel and flashed a proud smile. "He put on his red apron and matching chef's hat and went to work, cracking eggs and stirring batter. The end result was his first masterpiece. When we delivered the cake to my sister's house, he ran straight in and proclaimed, *I baked the cake all by myself. I'm the best baker ever."*

"And look at him now." Isabel turned to

Chris. "A master chef in his own right."

He slumped down in the recliner and hid his face behind his hands.

Isabel chuckled.

Mark said, "I'll tell you my personal favorite."

"No, Dad. Not you too," Chris whined.

"When he was two, we had this dog, Sparky. The boy and his dog were thick as thieves, and one day Chris decided to sample Sparky's food. He crawled to Sparky's bowl and started chomping on Alpo, like any good doggy would do. Sparky just sat there, looking at him, totally confused by what was happening. Eileen rushed in and grabbed up the Chris Hound, saving Sparky's meal, most of which was smeared all over the boy's face."

Isabel burst out laughing.

Chris stood from the recliner. "Okay, Mom...Dad, you've had your fun, but we should head out." The wall clock opposite the TV read eight o'clock.

"Oh, wow," Eileen said. "I didn't realize it was so late. Before you leave, let me pack your dessert to go."

Isabel joined Chris at the door. "Thanks

for a great dinner, you guys."

"It was great having you, sweetheart." Eileen handed Chris two covered plates of chocolate fudge cake. She gave Isabel a big hug.

Mark did the same, then opened the front door for them. "See you soon."

Eileen stood in the doorway and waved as Chris backed out of the driveway. "Sorry about my mom. She means well, but she can be a little pushy sometimes."

Isabel chuckled. "She's just excited that we're back together."

"Thanks for letting her think that." He smiled while keeping his focus on the dark road.

"You were such a cute kid."

"All kids are cute. I hope to have my own someday."

The silence that followed made him look at her. "Did I say something wrong?"

"We could've had kids already, if you hadn't left me."

"I know. I screwed up. When are you going to forgive me?"

"That kind of hurt never goes away, Chris."

He turned the car onto Isabel's street. "Look. I'm doing my part here, taking care of you, proving you can count on me. When are you going to do your part and start forgiving me?"

"My part?" She scowled. "I've been doing my part, trying to mend what you broke. You may think things are all peachy keen between us now, but it's not easy to erase six years of heartache."

"I just wish I'd never hurt you." He pulled the car into Isabel's driveway. "I'm sorry."

She shrugged. "Maybe you should go home, Chris."

"I'm not leaving. You can't dress yourself—"

"I most certainly can."

"Prepare your own meals."

"You brought enough entrees to feed a battalion."

"Besides, I need to change your bandages."

"You got me on that one."

"I can't go home and worry about you all night."

"Do you really think I can forgive you

that easily? Sticking around and helping out for a few days doesn't erase all the damage you did. Forgiveness doesn't come cheap."

"Okay. I get it, Bel." The hurt in his eyes said it all.

Swallow your pride, Isabel. He's trying.

Chapter 15

Isabel placed her purse on the floor of Dr. Anderson's office and took a seat on the couch across from her chair. "Thanks for seeing me." She made herself comfortable on the plush cushions.

"I'm happy to fit you in. What's on your mind?"

"Tomorrow is my first day back to work."

"I see," Dr. Anderson said. "Returning to work after a traumatic event can be difficult. You look good."

"I feel good, all things considered. At first, I had to rely on my friends and mother for almost everything, cooking, cleaning, getting dressed. I felt helpless, but with each week that passed, life's chores became easier for me."

"And being away from work for six weeks is a long time, especially for someone who loves her job as much as you do."

"It's true. I've missed my job a lot...but..."

"But it's where you met Ethan. How are you feeling about that?"

"I'm stressed about what my co-workers might say, the looks of pity they may give me when we pass each other in the aisles."

"You can't control what other people think. All you can control is your own response. Do you remember those breathing technique I taught you when we first met?"

Isabel nodded. "Both hands on my stomach and five deep breaths in and out."

"Excellent. Don't forget to use it if you feel overwhelmed."

"I've also been fearful of running into another psycho like Ethan. My response to that was to purchase a gun and sign up for self defense classes."

Dr. Anderson smiled. "Isabel, that's huge. I know how you feel about guns."

"It's a necessary evil."

"Whatever makes you feel safe. Are you sure you can handle a gun?"

"I've got Liv to help me there. She knows everything about guns."

"And how about Chris?"

Her stomach tightened. "Do we have to talk about him?"

"All in the name of good mental health. How's it going?"

"It's complicated. The last few weeks have been a roller coaster. There are times when I look at him and I think, *that's the guy for me."*

"What's the problem then?"

"I don't know how to get past all the pain and anger he left me with. Who's to say he won't do it a second time?"

"What about the risks we take for love? We talked about that."

"Yeah. Where my feelings for Greg were concerned. Look what that got me. I don't want to suffer like that again."

"I understand your hesitancy, but don't pin that on Chris. He's been supportive since your ordeal with Ethan, right?"

"He's been great. Even when I've tried to push him away."

"It seems to me like he's trying to prove himself worthy of you, Isabel. I know this is difficult, but I think you need to step out of your own way. Give into your feelings and see what happens."

Isabel sighed. "I wish it were that easy."

Dr. Anderson stood from her chair to walk Isabel to the door. "Good luck at work tomorrow."

"Thank you."

After she left the office, she headed to her car and drove straight to the gym for her first self defense class.

***

Isabel stood on the dark blue mat in the gym and surveyed the room: basketball hoops at either end, bleachers, climbing ropes, and tether-ball poles. The air smelled of sweaty pine cleaner. She counted seven women in the class, all waiting for the instructor. Self defense was big business for the YMCA. She wondered if any of them had also suffered a near death experience.

"Hi, everyone." A very healthy looking woman walked in, not an ounce of fat on her, like Barbie Doll on steroids. "My name is Erin and I will be your instructor. Today's class will be broken down into three parts.

For the first part, we will be practicing three basic self defense moves. The groin kick, the heel palm strike, and the elbow strike. You'll observe first, then you'll mimic me as I perform the moves again."

Erin stood firm. "The groin kick." She lifted her right leg off the ground and jammed her knee upward. "This is good for close combat. If you have a little room..." She kicked her foot forward, toes pointed down. "Right between the legs. Knee up, kick, knee up, kick. Three more times."

Erin made all the techniques look easy, but mimicking her was easier said than done. Isabel found it difficult to keep her balance. Erin moved around the class to offer her guidance as needed.

"Nicely done, everyone," Erin said with a bottle of water in her hand. "Take five minutes to cool down, then we will begin the next portion of the class: how to disarm an assailant with a gun.

Those words, *disarm* and *assailant*, gave her goosebumps. Her knees suddenly felt wobbly.

"All right class, is everyone ready?"

No.

If you ever come face-to-face with an attacker that is wielding a gun, it is important to know how to disarm him." She held her arm out. "Louie," she shouted. "Come in, please."

A tall muscular man walked in. He was holding a gun as he stormed straight to Erin and pointed the gun in her face. Erin moved so fast, her hands were a blur, but there was no doubt about it. She had Louie's gun in both hands and pointed at him.

Louie held his hands up in surrender.

The women clapped, so Isabel joined in.

"Now we'll slow it down for you." She handed Louie the gun, and he promptly pointed it at her chest. "Left hand to gun hand. Strike his wrist with your left wrist. This will shove the gun to the right, and it won't be pointing at you if it goes off. Right hand sweep to grab the gun barrel. At the same time, use a twisting motion to point the gun back at him. It'll wrench his wrist so bad he'll let go. Even Louie isn't strong enough to hold it. The gun barrel is now in your right hand, and the grip is free. Grab it with your left hand, let go of the barrel in your right hand and hold the gun with both hands."

In slow motion it looked easy. "Left to right. Right to left. Twist. Left hand. Both hands. I want each of you to come up, one-by-one, and take the gun from Louie. I'll help you as needed."

Isabel's stomach grew a pit, a heavy pit. Louie was convincing in his portrayal of the bad guy. He even scowled and shouted, "Gimme your money," or "Put your hands up."

Her hands were shaking. She turned to Erin fretfully.

Erin smiled and gave her an encouraging nod. "You can do this."

She took a deep breath and mimicked Erin's moves. *Left to right. Right to left, right hand twist, gun in left hand then both hands.* It surprised her how easily his gun hand moved left. The leverage was definitely in her favor. The trick was meeting that motion with her right hand going in the opposite direction and twisting the gun at the same time. It took a few tries to get the timing right. Louie was patient with her, and she could tell he was really holding tight to the gun. It fell to the mat a couple times, but finally she managed to keep hold of it and point it at Louie with both hands.

He smiled.

"Nicely done," Erin said. "Next."

The maneuver felt doable here in class, but she wondered if she could pull it off in the real world, against a real attacker, when her adrenaline was flowing and it was truly a life or death situation.

"Believe in yourselves, ladies. You'll get plenty of practice as these classes continue."

Believe in yourself, damn it.

For the last part of the class, Erin had everyone take turns sparring with Louie, who taught them three additional techniques: roundhouse kick, leg sweep, and sucker punch.

By the end of the hour-long class, every part of Isabel's body ached. She feared she wouldn't live through the month-long series of grueling classes.

"Good work, ladies. Remember. Believe in yourselves. See you Thursday. Check your schedules. Don't be late."

***

When Isabel got home, she kicked off her shoes, walked into the bathroom and stripped down for a shower. She closed her eyes as the stream of hot water soaked her long dark hair. She always found showers to be therapeutic. The hotter they were, the better she felt. She took the opportunity to practice. *Knee up, kick. Left to right, right to left, twist, left hand, both hands. Knee up, kick.* She felt as clumsy as an ox on a tightrope.

Finally, she forced herself to turn off the water, toweled dry, and dressed for bed then walked slowly into the kitchen, her body still sore from her earlier exertions.

Her phone rang as she was about to make herself a late dinner.

"Hey, Liv. What's up?"

"I know it's last minute, but I was thinking I could stop by with some Chinese food."

"Meaning I don't have to cook?" She laughed. "Come on over."

By the time Liv arrived, Isabel had dressed in shorts and a pullover. She spread the Chinese food containers across the coffee table, and they sat on a couple of pillows like they were in their college dorm.

"I have news," Liv said.

Isabel dug into the sweet and sour chicken. "Do tell."

Liv smiled. "Jack wants to take me on a weekend getaway."

"That's awesome. Where to?"

"Bushkill Falls." She clapped her hands together.

"I'm so happy for you. When?"

"Next month. I haven't been this serious with someone in a long time. I can be myself with him, and he's a cop, so he understands how time consuming the job can be."

Isabel thought of a great idea. "We should go on a double date."

"So things are better between you and Chris?"

"They will be."

Liv chuckled. "Whatever that means. A double date sounds great. What do you have in mind?"

"How about bowling? This Friday."

"I'll check with Jack, but that should work."

"I'm nervous about work tomorrow."

"I would be too. But all you have to do is get through the first day."

"One day at a time."

"Exactly."

"I just don't want anyone's pity."

"Their opinions don't matter. You know your worth."

Isabel laughed. "I wish I had your confidence."

"You do, just don't know it." Liv smacked her hand on the table. "We haven't read our fortune cookies." She fished them out of the bag and tossed one to Isabel.

Liv went first. "*Unlimited happiness awaits you.*" She grinned. "I like the sound of that. Your turn, Bel."

"I could use an encouraging fortune." She cracked open her cookie. *Keep your friends close and your enemies closer.* "What's that supposed to mean?"

Liv quickly took the little paper from Isabel's hand. "Nothing. You don't have any enemies."

"Sure. Yeah, it's nothing."

Chapter 16

The next morning at Fit Cuisine Magazine, as Isabel walked into the office, the lights flashed on and everyone cheered. A *Welcome Back* banner hung on the wall, adorned with an assortment of colorful balloons above a table of refreshments: doughnuts, chocolate crescents, and a variety of bagels.

Stan was the first to greet her. "It's good to see you again." He extended his arms for a hug. "We were all really worried."

"You can't get rid of me that easily."

Stan laughed. "You certainly haven't lost your sense of humor."

Maggie was next to greet her. She gave her a tight squeeze. "I never liked Greg, anyway."

"Yes you did."

Maggie let out a nervous laugh. "Alright, I did."

"It's okay. I liked him too. He had us all

fooled."

"I'm really glad you're back."

"Me too."

She walked to the refreshment table and picked up a Boston Cream doughnut. As she was eating it, one of her co-workers, Tim, tapped her on the shoulder.

"You know, most people just fake a cough when they want to play hooky." He showed her a roguish smile. "You really pulled out all the stops."

She nearly choked on her doughnut. "You caught me." And laughed. So far the day was going better than she'd imagined. No sympathetic looks or whispers behind her back. Just cheerful tones and playful comments.

"Okay, everyone," Stan called. "Time to start working."

She typed for an hour straight before she needed to stretch her legs. On her way to the water cooler, she walked past Ethan's vacant cubicle, and suddenly her heart started to pound, and she couldn't catch her next breath. The knife could have been stabbed into her stomach, again, she felt that much physical pain.

She rushed back to her desk, sat in her chair, and placed her hands on her stomach. Dr. Anderson's words came to mind: *Deep breath in, deep breath out. You're okay. You're safe.* It took a few minutes for her heart rate to slow and her breathing to return to normal.

No. He will not dictate my life.

She opened her desk drawer and pulled out her notebook. Then she took a pen from her desk organizer and began to write a memo to herself.

You thought you were powerful, that I was weak. But I'm here, and you're rotting in a jail cell. I won.

She ripped the paper from the notebook and taped it on her desk, next to her keyboard then she exhaled a calm breath.

Her phone buzzed with a text from Liv.

Still on for the shooting range after work?

She glanced at the memo then back to her phone.

Absolutely.

Liv had helped her pick out a Glock 26 from the gun shop she and her cop friends frequented. Isabel had packed the gun in its case earlier that day and placed it in the trunk of her car. She remembered what Erin had said: *you need to have confidence in yourself.* Today was as good a day as any to practice self confidence, though she had no idea what she was getting herself into.

***

Isabel drove into the parking lot of the *Watch Your Glock* shooting range. Liv had pulled into a space close to the entrance doors. Isabel parked in the empty space next to her.

While Liv waited, Isabel took her gun case from the trunk, her ear protection, and a box of rounds, and then they headed inside together. The owner led them to lanes THREE and FOUR. As they were following him, Isabel jumped slightly at the sound of gunfire coming from the first lane they passed. Hearing it in a movie was entirely different than enduring the sound from up close. Not to mention the pervasive smell of cordite floating in the air.

"Good luck, ladies." The owner turned on the lights over their targets, black on white silhouettes of a man's upper torso and head, twenty-five yards down the lane.

Liv gave Isabel a quick lesson. "Always point the barrel downrange, and never point the gun at anyone you don't intend to shoot."

Isabel removed the Glock from its case. The slide was open and an empty magazine lay beside it.

"Now you need to load your magazine with ammunition." She glanced at the box of bullets Isabel had set on the counter.

On Liv's guidance, Isabel used her left hand to hold the magazine and her shooting hand to hold the bullet.

"Set the bullet in the slot, pointy end this way, line it up with the magazine, and push it in with your thumb."

Isabel repeated that action. It wasn't easy to do, and her thumb hurt by the time the magazine was fully loaded.

"Good job. Now, insert the magazine into the grip and slap it hard to be sure it's locked in." She waited for Isabel to complete the task. "Last step. Pull the slider back to chamber a round."

Isabel had a little trouble with that. It took considerable effort to move the slider.

"Give it a quick pull backwards and let it go. The internal spring will do the rest."

Finally, Isabel chambered a round.

"Hot gun," Liv announced.

The more Isabel handled the gun, the more nervous she became. Now that it was a 'hot gun' she thought better of her plan to arm herself.

Liv continued the lesson by showing Isabel how to hold the gun, how to stand, how to brace for the recoil and recover. She made it look easy. "When you're ready to shoot, bring the gun up to eye level, lock your elbows, line up your sights, and gently squeeze the trigger. The gun will jump up, but in this stance, it'll come back down on target."

"Got it." Holding the gun felt like a reunion with an estranged relative: awkward and unnerving.

"Give it a try."

Ear protection in place, Isabel squeezed off a round. The bang was muffled, but the recoil startled her. The spent cartridge shot off to her right. She had no idea where the bullet went.

"Take your time. Make every shot

count.” Liv walked to lane FOUR.

Isabel kept a steady eye on her target, took a deep breath then squeezed the trigger. A bullet hole blossomed in the target, a shoulder wound. She huffed and fired again. White paper disintegrated. A little left, a little down. She pulled the trigger. A total miss. She fired again and again. The bullet pattern was scattered: one ear shot, a couple to the shoulders, a few on white paper, and only one to the chest before the gun quit working.

Liv walked over. "You're getting better, and you look more comfortable than at first. It just takes practice.”

"I’ll never make Marksman of the Year. I’m out of bullets.”

"Push this button here. The clip will fall out. Put your hand under the grip to catch it. Reload it again. This time, shoot like a cop. Two quick trigger pulls. We call it a double-tap. Focus on the chest area. We call it dead-center-mass. It affords the highest probability of a hit. Head shots are tough to hit, especially if the target is moving toward you. Pow-Pow. Double-tap. See if you have better luck.”

Isabel nodded. "Thanks." She loaded the clip, raised her gun and fired again. Two times. Keeping the gun as level as possible.

"Hold fire on the range," came over the loudspeaker.

The target came back to her via a cable track system. "Wow." A few bullet holes had formed a close-knit group in the chest.

Liv clapped her hands. "Nicely done. Good hand-eye coordination. How'd it feel?"

"Strangely good."

"To secure your weapon, remove the clip and pull the slider back to eject any round that might be in the chamber. Then look to be sure it's clear. Don't take anything for granted. Safety first."

She secured the gun and set it back in the case. "Thanks for your help, Liv."

"I expect you to practice every chance you get."

"They'll know me by my first name around here."

"Good. Now let's go. Jack's waiting for me."

"Lucky you."

Back at the car, Isabel put the gun in her trunk and glanced up at the shooting facility. Never in a million years did she ever think she'd be in a place like this, much less frequent it. She never knew she had natural eye-hand coordination. A real Annie Oakley she was. She just hoped she would never have to shoot anyone to save her own life.

Chapter 17

Isabel arrived home at 6:50pm. She headed straight for the bathroom to take a shower. Her hair reeked of cordite from the gun range, and she was sure her perfume would never smell the same again. She had a little over an hour to get ready for dinner at Chris's house.

Feeling like a new woman, she wanted an outfit that was comfortable, yet sexy, but not too inviting. It didn't take her long to coordinate that image: a mid-length, flowy black skirt and a light blue short-sleeve top with a deep-V neckline.

After she added her makeup and slipped into her black flats, she gathered up her purse and a light jacket, then headed to her car.

On the drive to Chris's house, she thought back to her conversation with Dr. Anderson. Ever since Chris came back into her life, he'd done nothing but show care and concern for her. He stuck around even when she demanded he leave. He deserved a clean slate, a fresh start, and they needed a new beginning.

When she arrived at Chris's, the door was open and he was in the kitchen, placing something in the oven. She couldn't help but check out his backside as he bent over. "Something smells good."

He turned around and met her eyes with a loving gaze. "It's either me or the chicken."

"My money is on the chicken."

"It'll be ready in about thirty minutes."

"Good, because there's something I need to say." She took his hand and led him to the living room couch. "I've been hot and cold with you for a while. We get close and I push you away, but you've never wavered with how you feel about me, and I finally realized that I need to stop living in the past."

"You're saying you forgive me?"

"I want you in the here and now." She placed her hand on his cheek. "I love you, Chris."

He could have been blown over with a

feather. "I'm relieved to hear you say that, Bel. I thought I never would, but here we are, together again, as we should have been for all those years. I love you and hope to spend the rest of my life proving it to you." He exhaled sharply. "And I want to start by giving you this." He turned to the end table, reached for a pretty pink box, and handed it to her. "Surprise."

She looked at the box with wide-eyed wonder. Judging from its size and shape, it could contain a tennis bracelet or diamond necklace. "What is it?"

"Open it."

She lifted the lid and couldn't believe her eyes: two tickets...first class to... "Paris? Oh, my God. Chris, this is amazing." Her eyes teared a bit. A trip to Paris would be a dream come true.

"It's two months from now, so we have plenty of time to brush up on our French."

She placed the box on the coffee table then scooted closer to him until there wasn't a molecule of air between them. "We're going to Paris." She threw her arms around his neck and let her lips find his. He gathered her in his arms and melted into her kiss like sugar in hot tea. Her fingers frolicked through his hair, and her tummy loosed butterflies to flit and flutter up and down her body. She shouldn't have denied herself these feelings for so long.

"Oh, Chris. I've been such a fool."

"You were being careful, and I don't blame you."

He slipped a hand under the back of her blouse and slowly caressed his way up to the clasp on her bra.

She felt a chill.

"Are you sure?" he whispered.

"Yes." Her heart began to race.

He unclasped her bra, and her breasts rejoiced in their newfound freedom. All caution flew into the wind. Every hurt feeling and angry emotion drained from her heart. They were together again, kissing and touching, the way they did back then, as if no time had passed at all.

"You won't be needing this." He lifted her blouse up and over her head then tossed it to the floor, along with her pink laced bra. His t-shirt followed and he pulled her in close again, chest to chest, skin to skin, hot and familiar. She delighted in his warmth and tenderness as their mouths explored each other and tongues tasted the sweet, sweet contours of their lips. Without breaking the spell, he lifted her from the couch and carried her up the spiral staircase to his bedroom. By now, her breathing had become quick and shallow, and a warm glow began to heat her insides and tingle her toes.

At the foot of his bed, he laid her down gently and let his eyes wander up and down her body. She kicked off her flats and closed her eyes to savor the excitement of his gaze, the want in the air, and the need to be loved in this way again. Lost in the bliss, she didn't know how he'd deftly removed her skirt and panties, but she did recall hearing the clink of his belt buckle and the unzip of his zipper. Oh, she wanted to look, to see him naked again, but she chose to let this scene play out as if he were her phantom lover, coming home to roost.

She heard him pull back the covers and slip under them, then pat the bed in a come-hither way, an invitation she could not resist. Now snuggled up next to him, she ran her fingers down his chest, over well-formed pecs and washboard abs. Yes, she was home again and wasted no time moving in.

In the aftermath, she lay by his side and let her heart rate slow and her heavy breathing recover. She knew they couldn't live in this moment forever. Life was unpredictable, sometimes great and sometimes messy. Right now, nothing else mattered.

The oven timer rang.

Except that. She giggled. "Talk about perfect timing. I definitely worked up an appetite."

"Let's eat." He pushed back the covers and got out of bed, revealing the full monty.

Yup. Exactly as she remembered him.

He picked up his jeans and hop-skipped into them. "Meet you downstairs."

"In a minute." She lay there wrapped in a world of fantasy, her every dream come true. A trip to Paris and a home-cooked meal after mind blowing sex with the love of her life, she couldn't ask for anything more.

Chapter 18

Isabel spent the rest of the week thinking about her trip to Paris. The more she thought about it, the more excited she became. The last trip she went on was to Miami with Liv, over a decade ago. It was a high school graduation gift from Isabel's parents.

In order to remain productive, she incorporated her daydreams into some of her assignments. Her latest one was *Top Restaurants to Visit while Vacationing in Paris.* She was particularly interested in having a meal and glass of wine at *Boutary.*

The article was halfway written when Stan walked into her cubicle. "I meant to give this to you earlier in the week." He handed her a printout with a long list of tourist spots in Paris. "While you're there, think about reporting on some of these. Use your expense account card. My favorite was the Eiffel Tower."

That was a surprise. Mixing business and pleasure on the magazine's dime. Priceless. "Thanks, Stan."

"You're welcome. Now get back to work."

After he left, she looked at some of the spots he wanted her to visit: Metiers Art Museum, Montparnasse Tower, Canal Saint-Martin. This trip was going to be amazing.

***

By the end of the day, her thoughts had shifted from Paris to her double date with Chris, Liv, and Jack. Bowling. How many nails would she break? Though bowling was her idea, she had a bad feeling that her night was destined to be a disaster.

After she pulled into her driveway, she put her car in park and walked to the mailbox at the curb. She pulled out a stack of envelopes, most likely bills and junk mail, then headed inside, plopped the pile on the table, and rushed to her bedroom to get ready.

As long as she was going to make a fool of herself, she needed something comfortable to wear. A white short-sleeved shirt and dark blue jeans fit the bill. Just as she finished tying her tennis shoes, the doorbell rang.

It was Chris. "Great timing." She let him in. "I just need to grab my purse."

"I can't remember the last time I went bowling."

"Me either. Should be a train wreck."

Chris drove and made her stay buckled in the passenger seat so she wouldn't pester him with butterfly kisses and wandering hands. When they pulled into the parking lot for *Deca Pins*, Liv and Jack were standing outside the entrance. They made a cute couple, overgrown teenagers standing side-by-side, their arms intertwined. He stood a little taller than Chris, sported a buzz cut. He had the square jaw of a cop and the brown eyes of a hound dog. Isabel couldn't help but notice how his eyes focused on Liv, even when she was looking and waving to her and Chris.

Chris parked and they hustled to join up with them. "We got here a little early," Liv said.

Jack grumped. "Her motto is 'if you're on time, you're late.'"

She playfully nudged him in the side.

Isabel chuckled. "Nothing wrong with that. Good to see you again, Jack." She gave him a hug then introduced him to Chris.

"Mackenzie, huh, that big shot restaurant fellow Liv's been telling me about?"

Chris accepted Jack's offered handshake. "For that, you're buying the first round."

"My pleasure."

Inside, Chris paid for the games. Bowling shoes were passed over the counter, tried on, and crappy house balls were selected. The rumble of rolling balls and the clacking of pins filled the air. Once they got settled in their assigned lane, "So, who goes first?" Chris asked.

"I'll go." Liv approached the ball-return, fingered her bowling ball, and stepped up to the line of approach dots.

"Get a strike," Jack shouted.

"You can do it," Isabel put in.

Liv looked back at her adoring fans. "Shut up. I can't concentrate."

Three steps forward, a smooth delivery, a curving ball into the strike zone...and with a crash, pins went flying. Nine down, one left standing. "Oh my God." She jumped with excitement.

Isabel and the guys let out a cheer.

"Go for the spare, baby," Jack shouted. "You got this."

The ball-return coughed up her ball. Liv grabbed it and lined up for the ten-pin. The delivery looked good until the ball curved a bit too far left and landed with a thud against the back divider-plate. The sweep arm came down and finished the job for her.

"Better luck next time, Liv." Jack was chucked full of enthusiasm tonight. "It's still going to be a hard roll to beat, but I'll try." He switched places with her, held his ball up under his chin, took a deep breath, stepped forward, and let her go. With a crack, all ten pins fell to their fate. He thrust a fist in the air.

Isabel and Chris exchanged 'we're screwed' glances while Liv glared bullets at Jack. "You totally played me."

He pressed his thumb and index finger together. "Just a bit."

After that, the night went downhill for Isabel and Chris. She sat next to him on the bench seat and rubbed his arm. "For luck, baby."

"Anybody for a beer?" Jack sang. "I feel like dancing tonight." He had no qualms against making fun of the losers.

Chris made better souffles than bowling scores.

Isabel made jokes of her gutter-balls. "Did you see how high that bounced?" She was having as much fun as Karaoke Thursdays in college. After game two, she got everyone together. "Let's take a break and get some chow."

Bowling alleys had the best burgers and hotdogs in town. And the French fries were to die for, lots of grease and salt. Who knew. Isabel ordered a round of heart attack food and selected a tall table that overlooked the lanes. Jack brought the beers.

"So, whose idea was it to go bowling?" Chris asked.

"Mine," Isabel said. "I had no idea Jack was a hustler."

Liv gave him a sideways glance. "He told me it'd been years since he'd bowled. Clearly he lied."

Jack laughed. "You'd all be broke if we

were playing for money."

"Number 107," came over the sound system.

"That's us." Isabel and Liv rushed to the short-order counter to get their dogs and fries. "So you two are really back together?" Liv asked.

"Two peas in a pod."

"Congratulations."

Isabel dug cash out of her pocket. "We're going to do just fine."

"Thank God that creep Ethan Bradley will be put away for good. His arraignment for murder is coming up next month."

"Hey. I took a chance, got burned again." She paid for their order, served in paper-lined plastic baskets. "But that's the risk we take."

"It's universal." Liv picked up two baskets. "Jack's a handful, as you can see."

"He's lucky to have you." Isabel picked up the other two baskets, and she led Liv back to the table.

Chris was laughing up a lung. Jack had him in stitches. Somehow, two full beers had miraculously appeared.

"Boys will be boys." Liv shrugged.

Isabel sighed. "My life feels normal again."

***

Chris dropped Isabel off at her house. He had to be at his restaurant for closing, help clean up after a banquet party. She kissed him goodnight, a peck was more like it, as they'd settled into a familiar relationship. The spark was still there, but after a night of bowling with Jack, she was too tired to light any fires.

When she got inside, she counted her broken nails, three, then spotted the pile of mail on the table. As she'd predicted, it was the usual junk mail, the power bill, and a curious envelope with hearts and happy faces drawn all over it, as if by a kindergarten child. The return address read: *Curran-Fromhold Correctional Facility*.

Her heart began to pound. Her knees threatened to fail her. She sat at the table and stared at the letter in her shaking hand. It had to be from Ethan Bradley. He was the only one she knew in any Pennsylvania prison. She was tempted to throw it away without reading it, but curiosity won out.

He's in jail. His words can't hurt me. What could he possibly have to say to me?

She took a deep breath, tore open the envelope, and began to read.

Dearest Isabel,

I hate how we left things between us. I never wanted to hurt you. I'm so sorry for everything and I hope that someday you can find it in your heart to forgive me.

I still believe that we are meant for each other, and the feelings I have for you will never change. You'll always have a piece of my heart.

Love,

Greg.

"Greg?" She couldn't believe how delusional he was. Did he really believe she could ever forgive him, or love him? Still, the letter shook her to her core. She got the phone out of her purse and called Chris.

"Isabel? Are you alright?"

"H-he wrote me a letter." She could barely talk, her mouth was that dry.

"Who?"

"Ethan...from prison."

"Seriously? What did he say?"

The alarm in his voice didn't escape her.

"He's still professing his love for me."

"He's a nut. Don't worry about it."

"Easy for you to say. He still thinks his name is Greg. Freaks me out."

"You should tell Liv."

"He didn't threaten me. What law did he break by writing a letter?"

"Okay." Chris sighed. "But if you get another one, it's harassment. Will you tell Liv then?"

"Yes."

"Okay. Get some sleep."

She hung up and thought to rip the letter to shreds but abstained from destroying evidence of his harassment.

She poured herself a bubble bath. The heat of the water, combined with the lavender smell of the bubbles gave her a sense of calm. She decided Chris was right. She needed to tell Liv about the letter. Maybe she could report him to the warden, get Ethan's mail privileges revoked. There had to be consequences for his actions. What was next? Emails? Texts? She had to put a stop to it before the harassment got out of hand.

Chapter 19

A month passed without another letter. It appeared Liv had solved the problem. Self defense classes were finished. Her self confidence had never been higher. She'd become a regular at the gun range and professed herself to be a master of the double-tap. Best of all, next month she would fly to Paris with Chris on a much-needed vacation, working or otherwise. As she drove home from the gym, she hoped Chris would propose to her at the Eiffel Tower.

After she pulled into the driveway and put the car in park, she got a call from Liv. "Bel, please tell me you're okay." Her voice was laced with panic.

"Why wouldn't I be? What's wrong?"

"Ethan escaped during his arraignment on the murder charge this afternoon, cold-cocked the deputy. The fool didn't even have him in handcuffs. Model prisoner, they'd said. I'll bet dollars to doughnuts he'll show up at your house."

Her stomach tightened. In that moment she wished her gun was in her hand as opposed to being in her nightstand drawer.

"We're headed in your direction now. Be careful."

"You think he's here?"

"We don't know where he is."

On high alert, every nerve in her body abuzz, she hung up and pocketed the phone. A quick breath later, she pulled the keys out of the ignition and got out of the car. The house looked as it always did, nothing out of place, but still, she armed herself with pepper spray from her purse.

Cautiously, with every step as quiet as could be, she mounted the porch, slinked to the front door, and checked the lock. All secure. She unlocked the door and stepped inside, her nerves as tight as a banjo string.

Living room clear. Dining room clear. She turned toward the kitchen.

"Did you miss me, Isabel?"

She froze.

That voice. It's him. Behind me. This can't be happening.

She swung around, pepper spray at the ready, only to see Ethan standing in the hallway. He wore a red prison jumpsuit, his hair was a mess, he hadn't shaved, and worse, he was pointing a gun at her. The moment of realization that pepper spray was no defense against bullets blew her confidence into the wind.

"Drop it," he demanded.

She jabbed the pepper spray at him. "Stay away from me."

He looked at the gun. "Glock 26. Nice. Found it in your nightstand drawer. Don't make me shoot you with it."

"How did you get in?"

"Key under the mat. Pretty stupid if you ask me."

"I'm not asking." Her heart slammed against her ribs. "What do you want, Ethan?"

"My name is Greg," he screamed. "Didn't you get my love letter? Didn't it make you want me back? Well, I'm back, baby. Now drop it." He straight-armed the gun at her.

"All right." She dropped the pepper spray, knowing full well he could now get closer to her. "Now what, Greg? You gonna rape me?"

"I love you. I came for you as soon as I could."

"You're supposed to be in jail."

"Yeah, well, shit happens, but I'm free now, and we can finally be together."

"Together? You can't get away with this. The cops are on their way."

He laughed. "Sure they are."

"No. Really. This is the first place they'll look for you. You better get out of here."

He stepped up to her, cupped the palm of his free hand under her chin, gentle as any lover would. "Then we don't have much time." He pointed the gun at her chest. "Pack a bag. I'm not leaving without you."

Left to right. Right to left. She pushed his gun hand left and came across with her right hand to grab the barrel and twist the gun loose. *Left hand on the grip. Both hands.* Lightning fast, she had him at gunpoint and double-tapped him, center-body-mass.

Chapter 20

Isabel stepped back from Ethan, the gun still pointed at him, even as he lay motionless on the floor. One move and she'd double-tap him again. She'd seen enough movies to know the bad guy always got up and attacked again. But this was no movie. Gunsmoke hung in the air, and the smell of cordite mixed with the coppery odor of fresh blood. It happened so fast. Her training had paid off. She was a survivor.

As she lowered the gun, reality set in, shock even, as she realized the gravity of her actions. She'd taken a life. A man was dead. Good man, bad man, it made no difference. Her hands began to tremble, her lips, her chin, too. A wave of nausea threatened to add the stench of bile to the scene. She dropped the gun and stepped back against the wall, crouched down to her haunches, and buried her face in the palms of her hands. "What have I done?"

The front door banged open. "Isabel. Isabel." Liv and her team had burst into the room.

She looked up, heard their voices, watched an officer kneel to Ethan sprawled on the floor in a pool of blood.

Liv found her, a crumpled mess, tears letting loose, her hands shaking. "It's okay, Bel. You're okay." Liv stroked Isabel's hair. "He's down. He can't hurt you."

The uniformed officer kneeling next to Ethan set two fingers on the side of his neck, and then shook his head. "He's dead." Another officer picked up the gun, cleared it, then set it on the table. Other officers fanned out through the house, checking rooms and reporting, "Clear."

Chris rushed in and knelt to Isabel. "Are you hit?"

"No."

"Thank God you're okay."

"I'm not okay. I'm a wreck. Look at what I've done."

He kissed the top of her head, then looked up to Liv. "Thanks for calling me."

"I was hoping you'd get here before us. If I'd known about this, I wouldn't have called. It's a crime scene now." Liv turned her attention to Isabel. "I hate to do this, Bel, but we have to take you downtown. Interview you, on the record. Standard police procedure."

"I understand."

"I know a good lawyer," Chris said. "Don't say anything." He looked at Liv. "Standard suspect procedure."

A uniformed cop placed her in handcuffs and led her outside. As he escorted her to a police car, she looked back to see Chris and Liv standing side by side on the front porch. Chris was rocking back on his heels, his palms pressed together and his steepled fingers touching his lips. Liv was frowning, one hand placed on her hip.

"It's okay, guys," she called.

He opened the door and helped her duck to get into the car.

The door shut and closed her in. As she struggled to get comfortable on the fiberglass seat with her hands cuffed behind her, she had an epiphany. For the first time in months, she wasn't worried or afraid. The black cloud that was Ethan Bradley was no longer hanging over her head. She wouldn't have to look over her shoulder anymore. She was free.

***

Isabel had been waiting in a holding cell for hours. Her head was bobbing and her eyes were fluttering. She finally gave in to exhaustion and laid down on the bench seat with her head as far from the toilet as possible. The sounds of distant voices and banging doors faded away. She found herself in a park, walking hand-in-hand with her dad. Sunlight dappled through the trees. "It's over, Dad."

"I know."

It was surreal, walking past his lifeless body on the sidewalk. She wiped tears from her eyes. "How strange that I'd meet your killer at work, that we'd fall in love. Ethan thought it was divine intervention."

"It was."

"What do you mean?"

"Isabel, you needed closure. He needed to be caught and punished."

"Wait a minute. You're the reason I met him?"

"He had nothing to lose when he

murdered me. I guided his life, gave him an education, a job, the love of his life. He had everything to lose when I pulled the rug out from under him."

"He damn near killed me, Dad."

"Yeah. I didn't see that coming, but you're a smart girl. I knew you'd put the pieces together, put him in his place, make him show his evil side again. And you're a stronger woman now, for all that you went through."

"What doesn't kill me makes me stronger?"

"Ethan is dancing with the devil, right where he belongs, and you're free to be with Chris, the man you were always meant to be with."

"Don't tell me you sent him to Ohio."

"He did that on his own, to be a better provider. Of course, he wouldn't tell you that. Enjoy your life with him, sweetheart. You've both earned it."

A few steps later, she no longer felt his hand in hers. When she looked, he was gone. "See you in my dreams, Dad."

She opened her eyes. She wasn't drenched in cold sweat or trembling with fear, but content in the knowledge that her father would always be there for her...and Chris.

Chapter 21

Isabel and Chris sat beside each other in first class, soaring above Philly in a wide-body jet. She sipped from a flute of champagne as she looked out the window. Below she could see fields of brilliant greens, forests that stretched for miles, and roads and rivers going every which way. What a beautiful world in which to be in love.

The DA had decided she'd acted in self defense. She was a free woman, in more ways than any of them knew.

She turned to look at Chris and smiled. "I didn't realize how much I needed this, until I stepped on the plane."

He took a ring box from his suit-coat pocket and flipped it open, revealing a rock the size of Gibraltar. "Will you marry me?"

"I was hoping you'd ask me under the Eiffel Tower."

"I can't wait that long. Is that a no?"

"Of course it's not a no."

"I'll take that as a yes." He took the ring from the box and placed it on her finger. It fit perfectly. He followed up with a kiss. "I think this calls for a toast." He lifted his flute of champagne. "To Mrs. Isabel Mackenzie and the risks we take for love."

She raised her glass to his. "And new beginnings."

As the jet banked to the east toward Paris, they toasted to their future and to whatever love might bring.

About the Author

Katelyn Marie Peterson graduated from Southern Connecticut State University with a bachelor's degree in journalism and writes freelance pieces for various newspapers. When she isn't typing on her laptop, she enjoys movie marathons, singing show tunes in the car, and cozying up with a good book. Katelyn resides in Connecticut with her husband and two children, a stay-at-home mom with a passion for writing Romance.

Also by Katelyn Marie Peterson

www.twbpress.com/californiabetrayal.html

New York City transplant Shay Collins is apprehensive about returning to California for her brother's wedding. She knows she'll cross paths with her ex-husband, the drunk, and Jason, her secret high school flame and brother's best man, and she's excited to see her dad, her rock, but facing her manipulative mother is her biggest fear. True to form, Mom's got her nose in everyone's business, but when her brother's ex-girlfriend comes to town, Shay learns the depths of her mother's evil doings, and from there, it only gets worse as more lies are revealed. The wedding is off, her drunk ex is hospitalized after crashing his car, and Jason, the sweet man that he is, can't help her put out all the fires, but when her dad dies suddenly, one final betrayal comes to light, and that one is unforgivable. Through it all, Jason stands beside her, and the flames grow higher.

Made in the USA
Middletown, DE
28 September 2022